good deed rain

42 Books by Allen Frost

...Ohio Trio...Bowl of Water...
...Another Life...Home Recordings...
...The Mermaid Translation...The Selected Correspondence of Kenneth Patchen...
...The Wonderful Stupid Man...
...Saint Lemonade...Playground...Roosevelt...
...5 Novels...The Sylvan Moore Show...
...Town in a Cloud...A Flutter of Birds Passing Through Heaven: A Tribute to Robert Sund.......At the Edge of America.......
....Lake Erie Submarine....The Book of Ticks....
.........I Can Only Imagine.........
...The Orphanage of Abandoned Teenagers...
...Different Planet...Go With the Flow: A Tribute to Clyde Sanborn...Homeless Sutra...
..The Lake Walker..A Hundred Dreams Ago..
....Almost Animals....The Robotic Age....
....Kennedy....Fable....Elbows & Knees: Essays and Plays....The Last Paper Stars....
...Walt Amherst is Awake...When You Smile You Let in Light....Pinocchio in America....
....Florida....Blue Anthem Wailing....
...The Welfare Office...Island Air...
...Imaginary Someone...Violet of the Silent Movies....The Tin Can Telephone....
....Heaven Crayon....Old Salt....

OLD SALT

OLD SALT © 2020
Allen Frost, Good Deed Rain
Bellingham, Washington
ISBN: 978-1-64764-425-3

Writing & Drawings: Allen Frost
Also some mysterious scraps found
on telephone poles and sidewalks
Cover: Leon Dusso
Cover Assistance: Jen Armitage
Apple: TFK!

"But the artist is vain. He can't destroy the beauty he's created."
 —*The She Creature* (1956)

"The artist in me wishes I could see what a nice job I've done. But I never will."
 —*Dark Passage* (1947)

OLD SALT

Allen Frost

Good Deed Rain ◊ Bellingham, Washington ◊ 2020

the Chapters

1 Inspiration	11
2 The Book	15
3 The Show Off	19
4 Ventriloquism	24
5 Together	29
6 Circled by Hadrians	33
7 Interview with a Moth	37
8 Meeting in the Alley	40
9 Dale Muldoon	45
10 Geppetto's Pizzeria	49
11 The Tiger	53

12 American Driving School	59
13 Irene daVinci	63
14 Hungry	69
15 Sleeping on the Moon	72
16 Another Sideshow Attraction	75
17 Breakfast	78
18 Carol	82
19 Old Salt	86
20 One of Many	90
21 Escaping	95

22 Midas Watts	97
23 Safeway	101
24 Gorilla Experience	104
25 Talking Pet	106
26 The Life of a Hungry Ghost	111
27 Cary Grant	114
28 A Brooklyn Tiger	117
29 John Wayne	120
30 Prayer	125
31 Every Bee	128

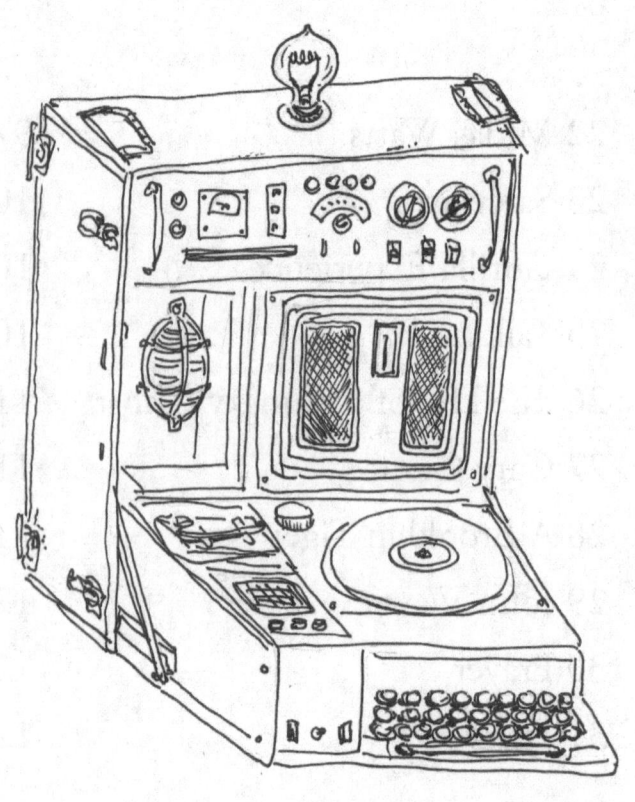

communication with another world

CHAPTER ONE

Inspiration

"Americans like our wars. We always have." I watched Herman Paxter say that on TV and I had to turn it off. Everyone should do that, but they don't and so you see his books everywhere. I'm partly to blame. I'm Don Wilson. I write those books for him. And now I'm working on another one.

Yes, there's a formula: the same old thing always sells. Paxter has his base, he knows what they like. Writing for them couldn't be simpler. But I was having a hard time. I didn't have the words. Correction: I didn't have *my* words for it. There were words, sure, but they weren't mine. It sounds confusing, I know. Let me explain. Follow me and you'll see.

On these streets are other people like me, going somewhere, hands holding up books to their eyes while they walk or stop for a light. It's rare you don't see someone with a book. We carry them with us everywhere. It's comforting; it's instant communication with another world.

The building I work in is a front for the office inside. Above the boarded up windows, you can still read the letters fading on the awning: Rex's Radio Repair. Our building is wearing a disguise. Rex is

Paxter's alias. That's a clue—if you know what to look for—an ordinary abandoned building on an ordinary American street. That's where an atomic typewriter and a stack of paper wait for me.

Forty minutes later and I was there, at my desk, staring the typewriter down. That machine was Paxter's only contribution to writing. His old Smith-Corona had been with him to war and back and he insisted all his novels be written using it. He would tell interviewers that his typewriter was his beating heart.

Poetic, right?

It's a portable typewriter, but over the years it's been updated and modified to be the machine it is today. Latched inside its blue metal traveling case like an oyster, I flicked the button and opened the lid. Sometimes the electric hum will spark something in me.

I listened.

Paxter's next book was in there somewhere. Once I gather some ideas, some characters, situations and plot spins, the Smith-Corona will roar into life, clacking out page after page. The problem is finding those words that will set this machine in motion.

The office was quiet.

There's only one other person in the room with me, on the other side of a gray wall divider. Wanda Ramone has been here as long as I have. She is the editor, with final approval before publishing. We've done four books together: *Imminent Contagion. Enemy Insight, Plot Command, Alpha Storm Rebellion.* All of them star Paxter's hero, Hadrian Beck. Who doesn't know him? He was already in 17 books when we started writing them and America can't get enough of him. More, more, more!

But neither one of us was looking forward to another one. Wanda even suggested we have Hadrian fall off a waterfall like the death of Sherlock Holmes. I think she was only half joking. I'm not sure.

I sighed.

The new book is out of my reach. I've been trying to find the inspiration, thinking it will come to me in a dream…aware they can appear out of nowhere…so all channels were open and waiting. Usually, anything that seems promising I jot down in my notebook. It takes a while to fill, before I feed them to the typewriter. Once I do, I never know exactly what's going to happen until the typewriter takes over. What comes out is only halfway my creation but that's okay. I've done my part.

This new book didn't happen like that.

Although I may not know where to start, ideas are finding me, odd messages like magic already written down. They appeared in the strangest places. A note was delivered to me by a passenger pigeon. One day at work a week ago, I bought a candy bar from the vending machine and this message was taped to it: *He throws his gun into the ocean.* I don't see how that could apply to Hadrian Beck, but I wrote it down. It was hard to imagine him doing that. After completing four books, I know Hadrian always had his pistol with him. The vending machine also supplies my morning cup of Luwak instant coffee. Yesterday, written around the paper rim was a message. It was another plot development. *Hadrian walks out on stormy sea to calm it and helps a fishing boat.* And there are more. Something strange has been going on. Little ideas like that have been haunting me. Reading them together, I could now see the book they would become. Herman Paxter's hero had been transformed.

CHAPTER TWO

The Book

Maybe worse than hearing Herman Paxter's admiration for war was what he said just a moment before in that same TV interview. He said his next book would be printed and available at bookstores tomorrow. That really put the pressure on me.

I released the platen and held my notebook pages hovered over it. I've had these ideas kicking around for weeks, waiting what to tell the machine to get it going, and here it was happening at last. I rolled my little notebook into the typewriter and it responded with a hungry groan.

I knew Wanda could hear the commotion on my side of the wall. She would be over any minute to see. I had time to fill the paper tray. The keys were already hammering.

"Hi, Don."

"Hi, Wanda, how are you?"

"Good! You started the book!" The pages were flying out. She was excited but I knew Wanda felt the same way about another one. I thought that we were done writing for Herman Paxter, that there was nothing more to say. She said, "I'm so happy you found your inspiration," and added with a laugh, "It also means we stay employed."

I laughed too. I didn't know what I started. I knew this wouldn't be like any other Herman Paxter novel. And I knew the old man would hate it. I couldn't wait to read it! I pulled a short stack of paper from the printer tray. More pages replaced those I took. This looked like another blockbuster. The Smith-Corona didn't make mistakes. It knew precisely how to take what you told it and turn that into gold.

Wanda leaned in close to read a page.

After *Alpha Storm Rebellion,* here was a change. It felt like the world should be with us on that. Hadrian Beck was over as a hero. If anything, he was the opposite. I never thought it would be possible to change him, but here was the proof, pouring out of the typewriter like water.

Wanda and I read that first page and stared at each other and we already knew.

"You did it," she told me. "You broke Hadrian Beck."

She was right.

All of a sudden I realized our job with Herman Paxter was over.

Wanda let out a laugh and pressed her hand over the page. "We can't read this here!" She pointed at the two photos framed on the wall. One was John Wayne, Paxter's hero. Next to Wayne, Paxter and his bulldog Cannon stared out of the glass at us. None of those eyes approved. "We have to take this somewhere else."

"I know a place. Have you been to The Last Exit?"

"Perfect! We can get a table against the wall. It's still early."

"Look at that thing go!" I said. Paxter's typewriter steamed. The light bulb was blinking like a summer firefly. "It's still printing!"

"I know, I know," Wanda whispered excitedly. "It's going to be another one of those Paxter tomes!' She seized the new stack of pages from the tray. "Once it's done, let's scram!" She dropped that thick manuscript on my desk and went to get her coat.

"I didn't know you like The Last Exit," I called over the wall separating us.

"I didn't know *you* did."

I smiled. "I'm surprised I never saw you there before."

"Maybe you weren't looking."

Maybe she was right. I didn't go to The Last Exit that often, a few times a week I guess and it was always crowded. Young people mostly, but also old men leaned over checker boards. It wasn't the sort of place I pictured Wanda Ramone; it was subterranean, loud and theatric. Then again, I was there too, an office worker in search of another world.

The typewriter coughed out its last page and the book was finished. I quickly gathered it all together and looked around my desk for something to put it in. I needed something bigger than the paper bag I brought my sandwich in. "How can we carry this dynamite?"

"Don't worry!" Wanda replied. "I have something!"

I switched the atomic typewriter off. Its shell was hot to the touch. "Should I take the typewriter?" crossed my mind. Its magic could make our lives better. We could use it on the run to make books of our own. Even after witnessing all the books it typed I still don't know how it works. How does its mechanical mind take my ideas and spin them into a formula all by itself? This was the first time those ideas had nothing to do with me, and with no regard to Herman Paxter's scripted world. I couldn't wait to see what this new book would be. All the days we joked about putting an end to Hadrian Beck, maybe the typewriter felt the same way?

I flipped the heavy stack of paper to read the title page just as Wanda came around the corner with a briefcase.

"No fair peeking," she said.

"I wasn't," I lied.

She placed the briefcase on my desk and unsnapped the latches. It looked like something from a spy movie, something in fact that Hadrian Beck might carry a million dollars ransom in. The manuscript fit snugly, hidden away as she shut the lid.

CHAPTER THREE

The Show Off

We walked to The Last Exit. It wasn't that far to Brooklyn Avenue, but as soon as we neared we realized we might have trouble. There are always a few people milling around in front of the café, reading or talking, but today there was a teeming crowd.

Wanda groaned. "I forgot! Today is their checkers competition." You would think it was Oscar night at Grauman's Chinese Theatre. We both knew we would never find a table. "That's okay," she decided, "We can go to The Show Off instead."

Of all the cafés in town, The Show Off is down on my list. "What about The Black Cat?" I pleaded. It was a little place, with Wobbly union posters on the walls, great soup and coffee that came with a free refill.

"Come on, Don."

I could tell from the look in her eyes where she really wanted to go. "Okay…"

As we walked past The Last Exit, I heard someone describe a checker move. You would have thought it was Willie Mays sliding home. Of all the times for a tournament, they had to pick this day…I stepped around the checkerboard someone had drawn in chalk on the sidewalk. They were even taking over the ground.

Wanda said, "Why don't you like The Show Off?"

"It's okay..." I remembered the last time I was there. A kid wearing a bowtie stood at the microphone and cranked out a riveting epic about camping, getting lost in the woods, going hungry and freezing and thinking he would die. Finally they sent helicopters looking for him. I thought it was over then he said he also had a song about it and before anyone could object, he was playing a mandolin and singing the story we already knew by rote...If only those helicopters got lost in thick mountain fog...

Wanda laughed. As if she read my mind, she said, "Well, I like it! It's entertaining. Maybe I should introduce you as the author of the latest Hadrian Beck potboiler! You get a free cup of coffee if you perform."

I made a face and she laughed as we stopped on the corner for the light to change. I was still trying to admit I didn't write a bit of it this time.

Someone touched my sleeve and I turned. "Would you like to buy some flowers for your lady friend?" A peddler shabbier than me held out a handful of dandelions. They don't last long out of the ground. These ones looked like they fainted an hour ago.

"Oh," I said, staying in stride. "No thanks, we're in a hurry."

"Too much of a hurry for flowers?" the peddler barked after us.

Wanda laughed. It's strange to see someone you

only know from the work routine, day after day, outside of the office in the real world. Wanda Ramone was like a different person. Laughter was rare at the office. There was nothing funny about Herman Paxter's world. "You would be a terrible bee," Wanda told me, "running past those flowers like that."

"They weren't good. They looked like they were run over on the street. You deserve much better than that." That was a compliment. I don't know where it came from. Being out with someone was exciting. A movie starring Don Wilson and Wanda Ramone was filming right now, right here on Lincoln Way, panning with us past Pacific Street, onto Boat Street, towards the ship canal where The Showboat Theatre was tied up. The sunlight held just right on Wanda through dappling effect of the sidewalk trees. If someone approached me with daffodils, I think I would have bought them for her.

We waited for a bus to pass then we crossed to Portage Bay where a Mississippi paddlewheel was moored. No crowd formed for The Show Off café onboard. Wanda was right; getting a table would be easy. I just hoped it wouldn't be too near the microphone.

She clutched the treasured briefcase tightly under her arm. It was worth more than a spy's ransom, to us anyway. I was still thinking of that page we glanced at. I knew we were about to be swept away. Wanda knew it too. As I reached for the door handle, she asked me,

"Are you ready for this?"

"I hope so." I opened the door for her. I recognized the Cornelius Barter song that was playing.

She thanked me and l ooked at the room and pointed at the small table at the back. I nodded.

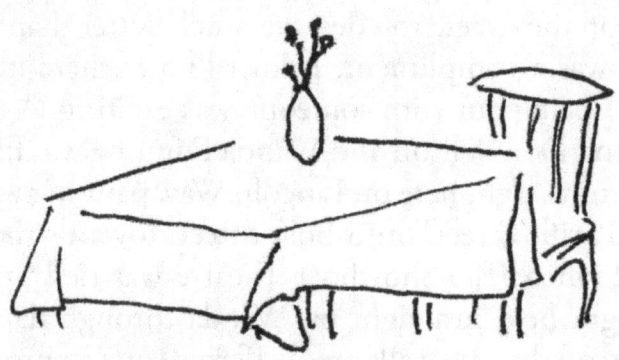

It was as far as you could get from the little stage. The microphone stand marooned all alone on stage. I hoped it would stay that way. Ghostly helicopters were still circling the air.

A couple sat near the front window, busy reading. A man in a tuxedo sat with his young son at the other table. I was a little worried to see a girl with a canary cage placed in the middle of her table. I hoped she wasn't waiting to sing a duet.

Wanda was quick to find her chair and she already had the briefcase opened when I sat down across from her.

"I want to tell you something about this book," I started.

"No." She fluttered her hands, "I don't want to know. It seems like you arrived possessed today, like the book just suddenly came to you out of the blue. I can't wait to read what you wrote!" She laughed at my not knowing a compliment. Oh, she was making it hard for me to tell her the truth. This book wasn't my idea. All I had done was gather what was left for me to find: it was already written down. I was about to tell her when she read the title page out loud, "*The Death of Hadrian Beck.*" She cupped a hand over her mouth as if a secret bird had flown out. "That's the title," she whispered.

"I know. I already peeked."

"You rotter! You told me you didn't!"

"I know. I'm sorry. I also have another rotten thing to say." That's when I was going to confess, but she wouldn't let me.

"Not now, Don. We have a book to read." Her attention was already on it, she held the first page, diving in. Soon we were drawn into the manuscript and synchronized like a couple of circus seals—as soon as she finished a page she passed it to me. We had a full teapot and I refilled our cups. They were still playing Cornelius Barter, a record I know by heart. Everything was perfect, waiting for the next page from Wanda Ramone.

CHAPTER FOUR

Ventriloquism

Then someone tapped the microphone. "Hello? Is this on?"

I turned to look—I couldn't help it, my concentration was torn. The fellow I spotted earlier, the one wearing a tuxedo, now stood on stage. Wanda put another page before me but it was too late, the spell was broken.

"Hello everyone. My name is Fes. It's good to be here. That's my partner over there by the window."

I looked at the table where I saw them before. I was expecting to see the little boy I had noticed but I was wrong. It wasn't his son. Left all alone at the table was a ventriloquist dummy. His painted eyes stared in another direction.

"He's ignoring me," Fes confirmed. "He doesn't want to entertain you. He's through with show business. That's what he told me. Can you believe that? After all these years I'm a solo act again." He sighed and stuffed his hands in his shiny pockets. "I need new material now…" His hand reappeared holding a folded piece of paper which he carefully uncreased. From his other pocket he took a pair of reading glasses and examined what he had written. "Let's see…" He leaned into the microphone, "Here's something I wrote on the way over here. An observation…Why do they call them seatbelts? Do they hold up the seats?"

Oh no, I thought and glanced at Wanda—he's doing standup comedy! She wasn't paying attention though—she was completely absorbed by the manuscript. Lucky her.

The silent room didn't deter Fes. "What did the ill-tempered cow say?"

Suddenly a voice from the audience answered, "Booo!"

I turned in my seat. It was the puppet. It had to be. It was glaring at the stage.

"Well, well, well," Fes grinned, "Look who decided to come to my rescue!"

The puppet guffawed.

I felt another page brush my hand. Wanda was leaving me behind. She was at least six pages ahead, she was barely here. She took her job seriously—she was a reader. A different world dreamed in her.

The puppet and Fes traded some more insults. I suppose there was a speaker carved into the little fellow's chest so it would seem to be carrying on this absurd conversation. I guess it was a leap in ventriloquism and maybe their technology would revolutionize the art. But they weren't saying anything new. It was just the same old tired patter. Still, much as I wanted to get back to the book, I was stuck listening to them. When they were done, my hands applauded out of sheer relief. The cage on the girl's table gave a shriek.

Fes bowed and left the stage, back to his puppet. The air was filled with a new song. I knew this one too. Mendelssohn. I listen to a lot of classical music on the radio at work. Everything is a soundtrack.

Wanda slipped another page in front of me while her eyes slid to the next new one she held. I had fallen hopelessly behind. There must be fifty pages dropped like leaves between our tea cups.

I said, "Wanda!" but she hushed me. Nothing was going to take her from what was happening in the book. Even as I gathered the pages she had already read, she shed another one next to the empty teapot. Hadrian Beck heals a bird hit by a truck. His hands folded over it like a paper airplane and flew it back into the air. I skipped ahead and saw him walk on water out to a troubled fishing boat.

I would need a lot more tea to catch up with her. I don't know why I let myself be distracted by that ventriloquist. I guess it's hard for me to concentrate with a puppet curdling across the room. Much as I wanted to start reading again—I was eager to see what would happen next to Hadrian Beck—I didn't get the chance. The next performer was making her way to the stage. It was the girl carrying a birdcage.

everything is a soundtrack

this place I took her

CHAPTER FIVE

Together

A half hour later Wanda and I were on a bench beside the ship canal and I was finally able to get back to the story. It just wasn't possible to read in The Showboat. For me anyway... Wanda didn't mind. That café was her second home. All the din of ventriloquism, bad jokes, puppets and bird duets was just the murmuring of TV in the parlor.

I prefer this place I took her. It was as far from the office as a distant planet. The long whisper of the willow leaves above us, a canal boat chuffed past, stirring the water to lap against the embankment. Apparently she could read anywhere. She held out another page towards me. I felt I could have found her a spot on a circus bleacher and she would take no notice. She was immersed in a written world.

Finally I was able to join her. I took the page from her and added it to the bottom of the stack I held. It could be an hour before I saw it again.

This was the first time I brought anyone to this spot. Funny it would be Wanda Ramone. I wasn't exactly getting away from work after all.

The new book was okay—don't get me wrong—my heart just wasn't in it yet. I had more to think about.

Wanda kept passing me pages and I kept watching the boats and birds. Way past the tree branches I counted the contrails scratching across the blue sky. Sixteen airplanes in formation. Their sound faded and I heard the ducks calling to each other as they paddled next to the shore.

Wanda turned another page over to me and I absently tucked it with the others. Then I noticed her hands were folded on her empty lap. She stared at the water too but with something else on her mind—she had finished the book. If the title was any indication, Hadrian Beck was dead and she was probably feeling that loss. After all, we had been with him for five books. Her earrings caught the light of the lowered sun. It was late afternoon, I don't know what time exactly but I supposed we still had some time before curfew.

"I can't believe you wrote that," Wanda said dreamily.

I took a deep breath and told her, "I didn't."

"You and the typewriter, I mean."

"No. I didn't have any of the ideas for it. I don't know where they came from. They were written down for me everywhere I went."

"Isn't that what inspiration is?"

"All I did was type up what I found."

We both watched as a yellow water-taxi went past. It sat low in the current like a bathtub. Now I had the whole book on my lap. I held it like a hen, or a baby

I found in a field of cabbages. The taxi sputtered away toward the locks.

"You know what?" Wanda said, turning to me. "Let's give it to the printer."

"I haven't finished it yet!"

"You can read it when it's published. Trust me. It's ready."

I shook my head. "What will Herman Paxter think of it?"

She laughed merrily. She already knew. And she wasn't afraid. "It's what we've been talking about. This book is the end of Hadrian Beck."

I glanced at the manuscript weighted on me like a ticking bomb. "Does he really die in it?"

"Better. He becomes a different person. He stops shooting and getting in fights and causing hurt wherever he goes. He becomes enlightened."

Now I laughed. From sheer amazement—I was picturing those 21 other books, the products, the toys, t-shirts and movies—everyone in America knew Hadrian Beck. Was everyone ready for a change?

Wanda opened the briefcase and we hid the book back in there. It wouldn't stay hidden for long. I wondered what Herman Paxter would be saying tomorrow.

He would blame us of course. As soon as the first copy was delivered to his door, he would explode like a rocket. All he needed to see was the title and it was all over for us. But I looked at Wanda as we walked beside the canal and I guess I wasn't afraid either. That sounds foolish I know, especially in light of everything that was sure to happen, but she gave me courage. We were in this together. Just like it says on that poster in the bomb shelter.

CHAPTER SIX

Circled by Hadrians

It was time to go back to the ghetto. Curfew was coming. Soon we would hear the horns warning us. The slums on 32nd Street weren't far away. You might think we would be wealthy from all those bestselling books. The fact is there wasn't money in it for us, the riches all went to Herman Paxter. Oh, we get some reward, sure, enough to survive.

We didn't say much. I don't know what Wanda was thinking but I suppose we were on the same wavelength, a little worried, a lot excited. I didn't even see what was on the way. Wanda did.

"Look!" she whispered. Her arm tightened over the briefcase protectively. "Here come Hadrians."

It was true. I was glad she spotted them—we could have walked right into them with our bombshell of a book. There were at least six of them ahead of us, crowding the sidewalk, dressed as their hero as seen in the movie *Instant Payback*. Those black leather jackets with red talon insignia must have cost them a fortune.

"Quick!" I breathed, "Let's cross the street." I grabbed Wanda's arm and tugged her towards the curb and as I did, in my excitement I knocked the briefcase. I tried to catch it—I had it for a second before it was falling. I wasn't quick enough to reverse gravity. I wasn't Hadrian Beck on the big cinema screen, twisting his way through a hail of machinegun bullets.

The briefcase hit the cement and split open with a crack, spilling out pages. Wanda was faster than me, hurrying to gather them while I stood there like a photograph. "Help me!" she cried and suddenly I was. I scrambled to catch the paper that had been thrown. I didn't look to see how close the gang was—I didn't want to know. Somehow we got the manuscript gathered together again.

"Sorry," I repeated, as Wanda shut the lid on the book. "I can't believe that happened." Who was I—Henry Fonda bumbling in 1941?

Before she could answer, a voice said, "You forgot one."

Hadrians were circled around us. They looked like they were ready to throw Billy Crystal off a rooftop.

Wanda and I both recognized the title page of *The Death of Hadrian Beck*.

Wanda said, "Oh!" and took the paper. She tried to hide her worry but I felt the same way.

We heard a cigarette match strike and one of the gang said, "What does that mean?"

"It's just a poem," Wanda lied, "a sad poem." She took a step away. "Don't worry though, it isn't true. It's only a poem nobody will see." I caught up with her as she moved, edging from them. A horse drawn cart clopped in the street and I tugged her with me off the sidewalk. We were lucky to escape. We would be doing a lot of that soon, but I didn't know that yet. We hurried along with the load of scrap metal. Some tin part chimed like a bell. At the next block we ran across the street around a delivery truck and Wanda had the key ready for Rex's Radio Repair.

I didn't see the gang tracking us but I gave her shoulder a squeeze. I was never more anxious to get into that nondescript lair of Herman Paxter's publishing empire. All we had to do was submit the manuscript for printing and get back to the ghetto before curfew.

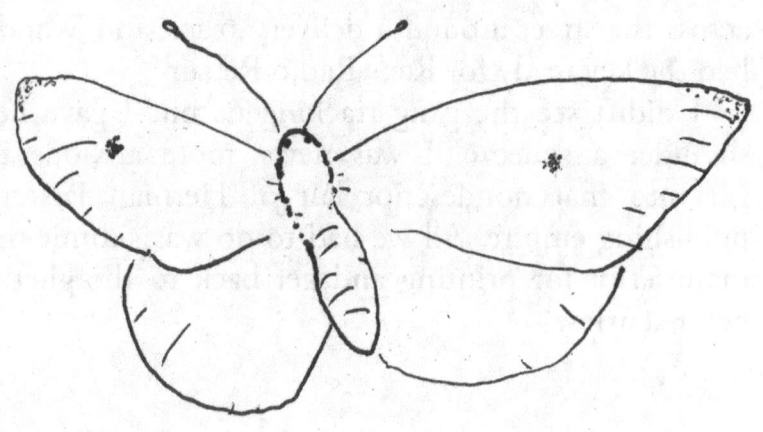

in the background of my dreams

CHAPTER SEVEN

Interview with a Moth

I said goodnight to Wanda just as the first sirens started. Before the second round of horns, I made it home. 32nd Street was crowded with people hurrying to their doors. A horse was getting parked in the alley. Above in the air, the clotheslines were reeling laundry inside. In the morning they reappear like flags.

Usually it's my alarm clock that wakes me up. Today it was a moth, yelling in my ear.

"Get up!" it screamed. The sound was tiny as someone screwed in a jar, a faint voice that could have stayed in the background of my dreams. It was the little velvet feet that woke me, as it crawled beside my ear.

I stirred, turned in my blankets and flicked my hand at the air just in time to see the cherry blossom shape of it flutter from me to the bedside table. It landed on the lamp and watched me.

I rolled towards it, "Were you saying something?"

"Yes! I've been shouting myself blue in the face!" It crept closer, across the curved lampshade. Stopping like a swan at the edge of the air, it leaned out and gave another gusty reply, "You're in danger!" Its white wings paddled to keep it from falling.

There was a time when it would have been strange to have an animal talk to you this way. Not anymore. Not since Talking Pet made it possible.

Now you couldn't walk past a duck without having to make conversation. "Hey! You like baseball? What do you think of our chances for the pennant this year?" For some reason that's all ducks want to talk about. They soon lose interest though—I don't follow baseball. They wander off until next time.

But I never had a moth tell me my life is in danger.

I sat up. "What do you mean?" I wondered if my voice sounded like a siren to those miniature ears. I whispered, "Why am I in danger?"

"Are you kidding me? We hear everything. We're all around you all the time. You have to get out of here right away. And call what's-her-name, tell her too."

"Who? Wanda?"

"Yeah, her. Tell her to wear a disguise, tell her to meet you somewhere out of the way. Do it now!" He was bossy for a moth.

But it had to be true. Pets were forbidden to lie.

So I did what he said. I called Wanda and she was just as surprised as me but we decided to meet in the alley two blocks from her apartment.

When I glanced at the clock on the nightstand, it still had an hour before the alarm would go off. "It's early…"

"Hurry!"

"Okay, okay…" I bumped around getting dressed.

I expected to be back, I had no idea what was on the way. As I sat on the edge of the bed to put on my socks, the moth fluttered over and I asked, "Do I need to bring anything?"

"Yeah!" his little voice barked, "Bring a tuxedo—you're getting the Nobel Prize! Hurry up!"

I laced my shoes and muttered. Of all the moths in all the rooms in all the world, this one flies into mine. "Why am I in danger?" I asked again. My coat was on, I was ready to go but I wanted to know.

"Herman Paxter sent a tiger after you!"

"Why—?" but I knew. The book hit the town like a bomb. I had to hurry—the moth was right. I didn't know why he wanted to help me though. I didn't have time to get the details.

"Go!"

"I am, I am! Okay, goodbye. Thanks for the talk."

CHAPTER EIGHT

Meeting in the Alley

I opened the door and left the moth in my room. I looked both ways, up and down the hall. Obviously, I was terrified. If there was a tiger after me that was bad, but worse was the thought that Wanda was being hunted too. We were in this together.

I didn't take the elevator. That seemed like the perfect place for a tiger ambush. The doors would open on the first floor with my skeleton leaning against the wall. So I went down the stairway. My footsteps clattered and echoed the chimney-like shaft, bouncing up twenty floors to the rooftop. Was I worried that a big tiger was pacing me, padding from above or waiting in the shadows where light bulbs burned out? If there are guardian angels, mine was working overtime.

I kept the pace, down, down, down the steps, got safely outside to the street, scurried like the prey I certainly was and I was gasping for breath by the time I arrived at our alley rendezvous. The laundry was already strung and blotting out the sky. A bright red union suit hung from pins. I checked the iron catwalk of the fire escape and glanced at other pouncing spots. Then I froze. Someone else was already in the alley—

hunched against the brick wall in a plaid overcoat—probably waking up from a cardboard bed beside that dumpster—no, I was wrong—as the figure turned, I saw it was Wanda.

With a grateful wave, I puffed towards her. When I kicked a can by accident, I almost jumped out of my skin. "I didn't recognize you," I said.

"You told me to wear a disguise." She held out her arms. The coat hung over her like a shadows. "Hey! You look the same!"

"I know. I was just trying to get out of my room as soon as I could. That moth was rushing me."

"What exactly did he say about us?"

"Herman Paxter is furious. It's worse than we expected. He sent a tiger after us."

"A tiger!" She even wore an old fedora. Where did she get that? Her grandfather? Anyway, it hardly hid her fear. "He must have *hated* our book."

I jumped. Someone behind us on the sidewalk passed by with their dog—it was the four feet I heard, the slight scratch of claws on concrete. "We have to get out of here, but where?" A window shook open on the third floor and I jumped again. "Come on, Wanda. Let's scram." Where would a tiger be least likely to follow? I took Wanda by the arm. She was mostly coat. Where did she get this disguise?

"Did the moth tell you where we could hide?" she asked.

"No. All he did was throw me out the door."

"A *moth* threw you out of your apartment?"

I laughed. "Well, it was a big moth." We were back on the sidewalk. We could take a streetcar, sit with the commuters, ride it all day and get nowhere.

An elderly woman passed us carrying a birdcage. The parrot eyed us and crowed, "You better get going!"

"This way," Wanda said.

And we were off.

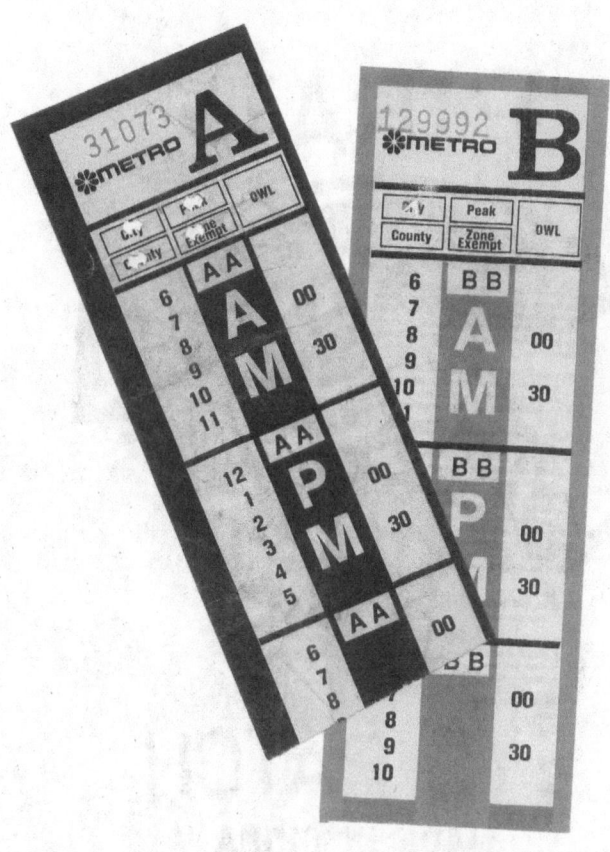

sit with the commuters

his one idea

CHAPTER NINE

Dale Muldoon

"*You* wrote the book?" I was standing beside the painting of a peg-legged sailor. More of him filled the walls and easels and leaned around on the floor like an audience. That subject was all Dale Muldoon could paint—that was his one idea. So how could he come up with *The Death of Hadrian Beck*?

"Of course not," Dale replied.

Wanda told me, "Five people wrote it." Then she added, "I wanted you to meet Dale first. He wrote the part about the magician."

That figured. I haven't finished reading the book but I already met the magician with the peg-leg. He appeared early on.

"Who are the other four authors?"

"A poet, a dancer, and a movie director. You wanted new ideas. I figured you needed some artists for inspiration."

"You needed a muse!" Dale Muldoon grinned. He held a paintbrush aloft like the Statue of Liberty.

The muses had done wonders for us. Now we were on a deadly predator's radar. At least Muldoon offered us his studio to hide in, long enough for the tiger to lose our trail hopefully. I turned my attention to Wanda and counted off on my hand, "A painter, a poet…a dancer and a movie director." I took a seat on a paint splattered chair. "That's four, I thought you said five people worked on it."

"Of course," she said. "I'm counting you too."

"Me? I'm not an artist. All I did was enter the ideas that came to me. Anyone could do that."

Wanda laughed. "Oh, Don…" She shook her head. With that fedora and heavy coat, she looked like someone listening to the Jack Benny radio show.

I insisted, "All I did was find the clues you left me. I'm guessing that was you, Wanda. Only you would know everywhere I would be."

"I learned your routine," she smiled.

"Well, I don't know how you got those notes in the vending machine."

"Yes, that was ingenious, wasn't it?"

"You went to a lot of effort on this book, Wanda, more than me."

Modestly, she said, "I played a part."

Dale Muldoon piped up, "You sure did! You got everyone together and made it a hit!"

"And now," I said, "we're running for our lives."

A phone rang, startling us all. I imagined a tiger stuffed in a phone booth, its big orange paws wrapped round the receiver. What did he want, directions to the studio?

"Excuse me." Dale Muldoon stuffed his paintbrush into his overalls pocket and followed the ringing sound. When he stopped near another portrait, I thought he was going to grab the telephone from the peg-legged butler portrayed in the painting. I glanced at Wanda, wondering if she was watching that too, when he found the phone on the floor and answered, "Dale here."

I pictured the tiger, talking with a toothpick in its mouth, half a sandwich held tight. An ultimatum was being delivered.

"Yes…Yes!" Dale Muldoon seemed to be happily ratting us out. "That sounds great! See you soon!" He returned the phone to the floor and clapped his meaty hands. "Guess what?" he asked us, but before we could answer or start to run, he continued, "I just sold two paintings!'

"That's wonderful!" Wanda said.

Honestly, that was hard to believe. I've seen one of his paintings for sale. It resides at Sinbad's antique store on Holly Street. And would you believe the price tag is $1000. The nerve of that guy!

"Just one thing," Dale said, "do you think I could get your help moving them? One of them is eight feet long!" He laughed. "They specifically asked for my biggest painting. And a smaller one too. What a day! Two paintings!"

Wanda said of course we would help him, Dale Muldoon was her friend. I only knew him as a name she sometimes mentioned. I didn't like the idea of going back out to the city streets. Did they forget about the tiger? Not me. I know it's out there, padding towards us, getting crouched on a balcony, it's tightening the noose. But the next thing I knew we were in the back of Dale's delivery van on our way to Geppetto's Pizzeria.

CHAPTER TEN

Geppetto's Pizzeria

I was holding an outrageous painting the size of a kitchen door. Lucky for me I didn't have a window in the back of the dim van. I would have been searching the passing streetlamps and the boulevard storefronts. A tiger would be up high, following the rooftops. Ahead of me, in the passenger seat, Wanda held the other painting on her lap, another Dale Muldoon masterpiece—"Still Life with Peg-Leg."

The van clunked to a stop and Dale popped outside. Wanda got out carefully on her side, holding her painting like a treasured sheet cake. I got a handle on my painting while I waited for Dale to open the back doors. The latch clicked. Hit with the sudden blast of sunlight, I nearly dropped the painting. That would have been painful—Dale's paintings are all done on wood. I probably really *was* holding a door.

"That's it," Dale directed me as he backed me out of the van. "Easy does it...careful..."

All the clouds seemed painted and the sun was shining on me like a spotlight. When the sun warmed you it felt like everything was going to be alright. If only I could lay the long painting down like a stretcher and take a nap on it. Then I realized that would make me look like a tiger's buffet. I had to stop and rearrange my hold. I wondered if Dale sold his paintings by the pound.

"This way," Dale said and swept by.

Over my shoulder I could see Wanda holding the restaurant door open for me. Dale bustled past her. He had an entrance to make, the famous painter Dale Muldoon, followed by two devotees. I heard Dale bellow inside, "Hello!"

I saw Wanda for a second as I tipped that airplane wing of art through the doorway. I was glad she found my distress amusing. "Which way to the bonfire?" I wheezed.

Dale called me from across the room and I felt another pair of hands take hold of my cargo. A kid in a white stained apron had the other end. "Thanks." We navigated among tables and chairs and flew over a potted jungle plant, barely clearing it. Dale waited for us with the manager. I soon discovered why the establishment wanted Dale's biggest picture. The wall was splattered.

The manager caught my look and explained, "The chef lost his temper last night and threw a pot of spaghetti. Pow! What a mess!" Red sauce right across the wallpaper, no amount of swabbing would clean it off.

With the manager's help, we guided Dale's painting onto two nails and that was it—you would never know what lurked behind the peg-leg sailor. We all took a step back and observed it like viewers in a museum. Then the kid in the apron picked up a tub of dirty dishes and left for the kitchen sink.

Wanda said, "Where would you like this small painting?"

"Oh—" the manager turned towards her. He pointed at an oily patch where a salad bowl hit the wall. "That's for the side dish."

a living excitement

CHAPTER ELEVEN

The Tiger

I didn't want to take any more chances. I told Wanda we had to go, we couldn't stand around while Dale Muldoon dickered with the restaurant manager. I wanted to wait in the van and we got as far as the sidewalk when Wanda spotted a bookshop across the street. People formed a line half a block long winding into it. "Look!" she said, "They're buying our book!" It was true—the window was stacked with copies—what was Herman Paxter mad about? Books were selling out the door! Wanda grabbed my hand and pulled me across the street.

Was I worried about dagger sharp claws and orange stripes? Not me. Not at the moment. We ran around a complaining donkey, a bicycle laden with laundry bags, the cardboard motor struggling to keep its frail rider afloat. It was a normal street. And I was like her, always excited to see our next book.

Years before, circuses used to roll into town. I remember those nights I was a boy and the big tents billowed next to us in the ticket line, calliope and the shrill games of chance. They created a living excitement like electricity hung in the air. These sidewalks had a little of that old feeling. I forgot what a big deal

Hadrian Beck was. These fans were standing out here since dawn.

Wanda bent closer to me, "Everyone's talking about the book!" I could tell she just wanted to float among everyone and listen to them and observe every detail the way you do when you watch a movie you love. I understood. But I was also keeping watch for the tiger.

Wanda turned and she was smiling happily, "Isn't this great!"

She was right. For the first time I wondered, What if there isn't a tiger? What if that moth was pulling my leg?

But it wasn't.

Between two people reading in line, a view formed of the bakery behind them. Centered in the window, all alone at a table, there was the tiger.

I couldn't move. Wanda walked on ahead of me, oblivious. I was frozen to the cement.

The tiger used both paws to tear a donut in half. It brushed a piece across the surface of a steaming coffee mug and stuffed the pastry in its mouth. Gulp. He wasn't in any rush. Clearly he was enjoying the shop, sampling their wares. The table was piled with dishes, some with pie or cookies, other plates were only crumbs.

I watched him dab at his fangs with a napkin as he reached for another bite.

That's when my adrenaline finally kicked in.

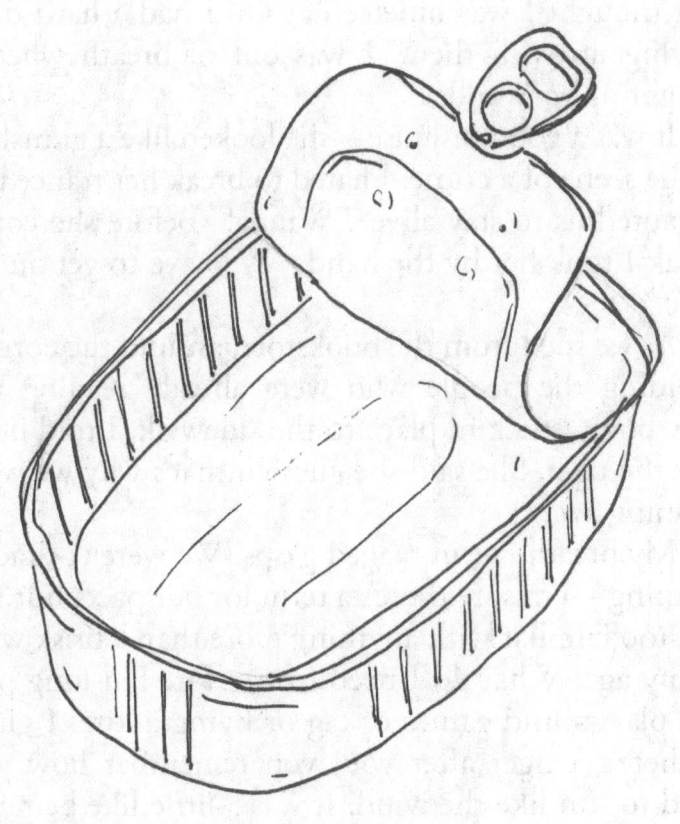

sampling their wares

I ducked behind the shoulders of jackets and sweaters. I may not be as fast as I used to be but my feet thought I was nineteen again. I had a hard time staying up with them. I was out of breath when I caught up to Wanda.

It was a good disguise—she looked like a gumshoe at the scene of a crime. I hated to break her trance but I wanted us to stay alive. "Wanda!" Before she could speak I took her by the hand. "We have to get out of here."

As we sped from the bookstore, around the corner, avoiding the people who were already reading the new book, stuck in place to the sidewalk, I told her I saw the tiger. She said she guessed that's why we were running away.

My breath cut in ragged gasps. We weren't exactly running—I'm sure there's a term for our pace, but I'm not too familiar with anything more than a brisk walk at my age. What do I need to run for? I'm long past the playground games of tag or flying a kite. I guess if there's a tiger after you, you remember how you used to run like the wind. It was a little like being in a dream, when it feels like the air is pushing against you, when you're dipped in glue. We crossed Boat Street and could see the blue water sparkling. Only yesterday we sat on a bench not far from here, reading the book that would change our lives.

To my relief, Wanda said she needed to rest. That was music to my ears. We couldn't have gone any further unless we rolled.

Wanda fanned herself with her fedora. I liked her windswept hair. Her face was flushed. I probably looked like a maniac—I could feel the sweat on my back. I took a deep breath. Did I have the bends?

Wanda asked, "Did he see you?"

"Who?"

"The *tiger* of course."

"No...I doubt it...only saw him a second...In a store." I wiped my sleeve across my forehead.

"That tiger's crafty. How did he know we'd be here?"

I shook my head. Did someone tip him off? Was it that wheeler-dealer Dale Muldoon?

American Driving School

- Teen and Adult Classroom lessons

- Teen and Adult Driving lessons

Learn how to drive with our licensed instructors both in the classroom and behind the wheel.

a hurry to get somewhere

CHAPTER TWELVE

American Driving School

I didn't have any more time to ponder—a car window unrolled beside us, a red sedan parked at the curb. "You need a ride somewhere?" a man asked from the car. Painted on the driver's door was: American Driving School. "I got a student driver here who could use a little practice."

A frightened girl sat staring fixedly at the dashboard. She looked like she had been roped to the wheel. This couldn't be a good idea, I thought, but Wanda said, "Sure."

It beat running.

We got in the backseat. The black vinyl and springs creaked. It was a tight fit. Wanda pressed next to me.

The driving instructor said, "You look like you're in a hurry to get somewhere."

Wanda said, "Yes, but we ran out of steam."

"Well, Thelma here would be glad to drive you wherever you need to go."

"That's terrific!" Wanda clapped.

The girl at the wheel jumped.

"Within reason!" the driver told Wanda. "We can't drive you to the moon." They laughed. Wanda seemed fine with whatever was happening to us. She was trusting, while I had grown to see everything in terms of a Hadrian Beck plot. Usually this was something I would write down, the beginning of an ominous scenario.

Thelma started the car. Her voice quavered, "Is it safe? What do I do?"

"Just steer us gently into the road," the teacher said. "After you make sure the coast is clear."

The car jerked into gear.

"Is it clear?" she asked.

"You tell me," he said. He kept his foot on the brake.

She clung to the steering wheel. "I don't know."

"Then look."

The car shuddered ahead as she let go of the brake and turned to look over her shoulder.

We all snapped forward as the instructor slammed his set of the brakes. I caught Wanda by the overcoat.

Thelma's reedy voice hitched, "I'm sorry!"

"It's okay…You almost had it."

A cart full of peat rocked by, narrowly missing a collision with us.

The instructor continued, "Let's look first, and *then* drive."

"Look first, then drive," Thelma repeated.

"Correct." He was holding a clipboard. The page clipped to it was a mess of red ink.

Thelma's face appeared in the rearview mirror briefly, like someone in a porthole of the Titanic. "All clear," she whispered.

"Did you warn traffic with your turn signal?"

She twitched. "No."

"Now would be the time to do so, Thelma."

I sat back. We were shanghaied. This was going to be an all-day event. I kept an arm braced against the seat in front of me though—I wanted to be ready for that brake. I quietly asked Wanda, "Where do we want to go?"

Wanda didn't seem to know. I hoped it wasn't back to Dale Muldoon.

Thelma began to slowly bring us into the road. The car could have poured from a watering can.

An ostrich stood on the corner watching us, a cigarette perched in its beak, one long leg casually crossed over the other while it leaned against a signpost and watched us. A sunny day like today and this was how that bird was spending it. I was glad we couldn't hear what the ostrich muttered—our windows were up and poor Thelma was already too afraid to notice. I ignored the ostrich too. Let it watch, let it judge, we were doing fine, rolling along like a tortoise shell. Emboldened, I said, "You're an excellent driver, Thelma. Keep up the good work." Wanda smiled at me. I don't even know if Thelma heard me, her every sense was keyed to the car. I went back to looking out the window. A slow-motion movie stretched.

"Where would you like to go?" the instructor asked.

"Home," Thelma answered suddenly.

"Not you, Thelma. I was asking our guests."

"Northlake Way is fine," Wanda decided. "That's not far away."

Not at this rate, I thought. The end of the block could be Chicago. What was on Northlake Way? It was all industrial, docks and cargo ships and warehouses...I hoped Dale Muldoon didn't have another studio there.

CHAPTER THIRTEEN

Irene daVinci

I waded through a sinking ship, carrying a cardboard box. Wanda's friend—the poet she knew who also wrote part of *The Death of Hadrian Beck*—lived on a canal boat.

We had the good fortune of arriving just as it was sinking.

Irene daVinci was running in and out of the hatch, piling her belongings on the shore.

I knew Irene from The Show Off. It might seem that I go there a lot. Okay, sometimes I do. It's on my way to wherever I'm going and once in a while I just need a cup of coffee. The café's entertainers are memorable, that much is true. And I like playing the jukebox when I'm there. They have a good one. Lately I've been dropping quarters for the old Country Western singers.

The three of us were able to empty the boat and we found the place where the water was coming in, a hole near the bow that we stuffed with a blanket and managed to slow the flow. Irene was lucky this didn't happen out on Puget Sound. There were plenty of shipyards along Northlake Way and she called to have her boat towed to one.

I sat on a chair by a box full of notebooks and videotapes. I had my pants rolled up over my knees and my shoes were drying on the rail in the sun. Wanda finally got around to telling Irene why we were here, about the book, about the tiger and how American Driving School dropped us off at her wet doorstep. Listening to the buzz of them talking I felt sleepy. I felt like the peg-leg sailor in that painting at Geppetto's. If I let myself go, I could drift away.

The tide came and went, low then high, and I am part of it too, pulled by the moon back and forth. The sun shined on me warm as a blanket. If I let myself go, I will drift away. I don't know where I am going or when it will happen or how. Painted to a board, eyes closed, I listen to the water. I hear a seagull too...and another. They circle the harbor. I'm floating up there with them, peacefully.

"Don!"

I was awake.

Wanda was hovering over me. "You were sleeping." For some reason, that delighted her. I suppose I understand—I would feel the same way if I caught her asleep in the sun.

"Irene is gone. They took her boat and everything."

"We haven't had much luck with our muses, have we?" I sat up and looked around and my survival instincts took over. "We have to make a plan. What are we going to do about the tiger? Do we trap it somehow? Do we jump on the next train out of

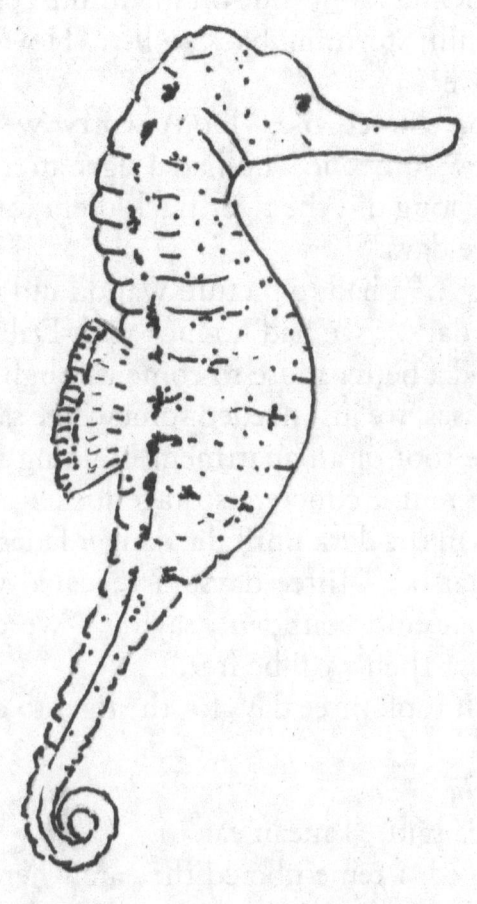

the tide came and went

here?" I felt more like Hadrian Beck than I usually do. He spent a lot of time on my mind. All this action brought him storming back to life. "How much time do we have?"

Wanda calmed me. "Don't worry, we have time. Irene knew someone who had a tiger after them."

"How long did the tiger track them for?"

"Three days."

"Okay…" I had to picture Wanda and me running for three days…We had no luck with Dale or Irene—we needed a better muse to come through. No, forget about muses, we just needed somewhere safe we could hide. The roof of an apartment building might do… or do we rent a concrete storage locker and padlock ourselves in the dark until the danger fades? How long would that be? "Three days," I repeated with a sigh. I tried to sound confident, saying, "We can make it three days. Then we'll be free."

"No. It took three days for the tiger to catch Irene's friend."

"*Catch?*"

Wanda said, "I mean eat."

I winced. I remembered the café where I saw that tiger eating. It devoured at leisure. "Yeah," I said, "we need a plan." I looked for my shoes.

"Irene left us a rowboat. We can paddle offshore. Irene said a tiger won't go out that far."

I nodded, "Right." That made sense. My shoes were still damp but I guess they'll stay that way as long as we're living in a rowboat.

"Oh—" Wanda offered me the bundled green army jacket she was holding. "Irene wanted you to have this for a disguise. And…" she turned it around, "look at the back." A square patch of white cloth with black letters spelled: **BECK**. "I don't know if that's meant to be ironic."

I took the coat from her but I was unsure, "I don't know…" If I needed a disguise, I could think of a better one. "What if you wear this coat and I wear yours?" I liked her old plaid overcoat. I had my eye on it all this time.

"Okay." She seemed happy to be free of it.

"Thanks." It fit nicely over my sweater. You would have thought it was made for me. And with the sun going down, I was glad it was warm.

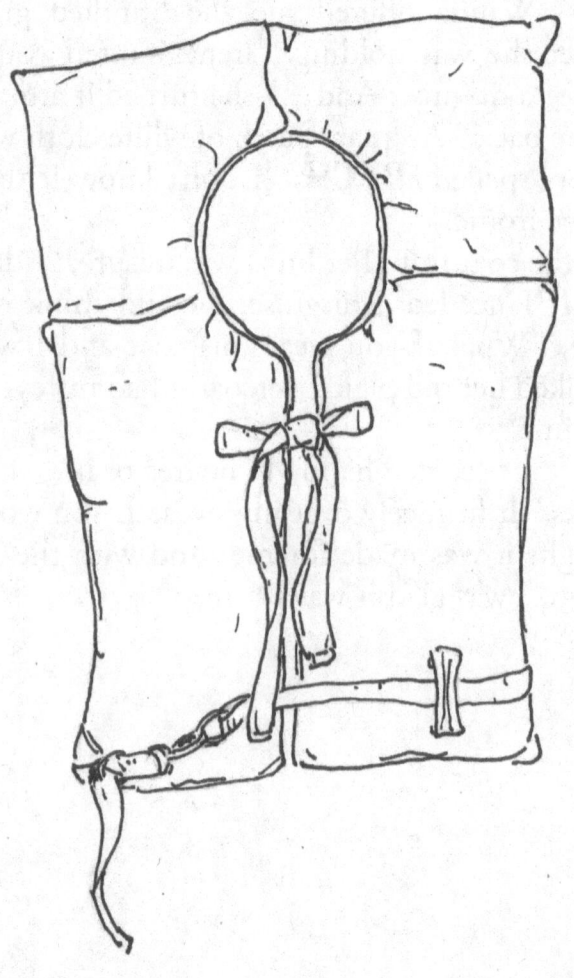

when someone says rowboat

CHAPTER FOURTEEN

Hungry

I followed the Beck patch as Wanda led me to the water's edge. When someone says rowboat, it's easy to get the wrong impression. I was expecting a Mother Goose bathtub that we would sit in knee to knee and paddle with big wooden spoons. "That's not a rowboat," I said. "That's a dory." I know my watercraft from all the nautical research I did on *Imminent Contagion*. A dory was much better, and bigger than a rowboat. It had plenty of room for us.

I took a quick look behind us—if that tiger was sneaking up, we still had time to dive on board. There was nothing you wouldn't expect to see in a parking lot full of fishing nets and boats in dry dock.

"Are you coming?"

I knew the difference between a rowboat and a dory, but if I sound like I'm Hemingway's *Old Man and the Sea*, don't believe it. I've used oars before, but only at the park on a duck-shaped paddleboat. Getting into our new home was like stepping into a trombone case. Once we were settled though, it was okay, with Wanda up in the bow and me on rowing duty, as we cast off and began our new life on the water. I'm no mariner but I guessed it would start getting dark in another hour. If we were in the middle of the lake, we would only be a dot to a telescope on shore. That's how I pictured the tiger, sitting on a bench, combing the waves with a spyglass.

I stopped rowing and let the boat settle into the glassy reflection of sky. We were safe from the tiger, out deep…safe as long as he didn't rent a submarine.

I turned around and told Wanda I knew the tiger's weakness. For what it was worth.

"Well, what is it?"

I said, "He likes pastries."

She laughed. "Just like Herman Paxter!" More than once we had seen him go through an entire box of donuts.

"It's true. When I saw the tiger in the café, his table was cluttered with pastries. I think we could use that to our advantage somehow."

"Somehow…"

I could have typed that into the machine back at the office and it would have been woven into the plot. "If only we could stock a cage with pies and fresh brewed coffee. He wouldn't hesitate to trap himself."

Wanda laughed again. "Now you're making me hungry."

"Me too," I admitted. Neither one of us had eaten. "Isn't there supposed to be a diner out here?"

"Yes, and a post office, a movie theater and a racetrack for the seahorses."

"No, I'm serious. I heard about it. It's on a barge

anchored around here." Our boat could have been marooned in blue paint. "Let me know if you see it, your eyes are better than mine." I turned so I could row again. Night was on its way. It took another hour for the shadows to fall, when the lights went on around the lake by the hundreds. I thought about us sleeping under a starlit sky, lying along the beam. It could have been romantic. I bet that would be a good scene for Hadrian Beck. I didn't have to think about him anymore but I still did. Did I actually miss working on those books? Couldn't we have gone on with that steady routine? Was it better being chased by a tiger into the middle of a lake? I was about to ask Wanda when she said, "Look! Is that it?"

I rested the oars and turned around. It was just as if we ordered it. Colored lights strung in the rigging made it look like a fairground ride. A welcome sight…

As long as I didn't get my feet wet again.

CHAPTER FIFTEEN

Sleeping on the Moon

So how did we go from floating on a lake to sleeping on the moon? Was someone writing our story the way I used to do, feeding a few words into a typewriter to see where they would go?

I followed her Beck jacket as Wanda was helped on board by someone she knew. "Euripides!" She turned and introduced me to the man holding a mop with his other hand. "Don, this is Euripides Newton. He works for Dale Muldoon."

"*Works*," he repeated, turning the word into an upside down sound.

I said, "We were at his studio today."

"Did you see my painting?"

"Which one? We saw a room full of them."

"Yes, I painted all of them." Euripides turned his mop into a paintbrush and swept a spot on the deck. "But they're not worth anything until his name is signed in the corner."

"Two of them now hang in a pizzeria," I told him.

"Which ones?"

Wanda and I looked at each other.

"A couple of peg-legs." I said.

She clarified, "A still life and a larger work."

"A sailor," I explained, "with a peg-leg."

Euripides shrugged. "That's how you know it's a Dale Muldoon. Even though it's not..."

Wanda and I traded looks. Sad to say, we knew how he felt. Our work for Herman Paxter wasn't all that different. We had Hadrian Beck to write—Euripides had a peg-leg to paint.

A clanging surprised us and Euripides translated, "That's two bells. I have to go. Enjoy your dinner." He picked up his bucket and stuffed the mop in the dirty water. He was off to make his living, swabbing the deck. We said our goodbyes.

It wasn't a big boat but they kept him busy, a bell was always ringing. We didn't see him the rest of the night until we were ready to leave. There he was, waiting at the ladder that led to our dory. It tipped about in the moonlight. Other boats were strung to it like cars in a parking lot.

Wanda asked Euripides if he knew somewhere we could anchor for the evening and he said sure. Once all the customers were gone, the diner would steam back to land. He said we could buckle ourselves to the buoy.

So we did.

As we slipped past it, I reached into the cold flow and caught the tie line. A simple reef knot and we were pinned to the lake. Yes, another reminder from *Imminent Contagion*. That was the first book we worked on together, Wanda and I. We have been conspirators since then, enjoying each other's company of course but never knowing we would be sharing the wooden bed of a keel. Somebody somewhere unseen must have typed that into our plot.

We used our coats for blankets. We listened to the patting water on the hull. Trying to count even half the stars we could see sent me dropping like a stone deep into sleep. No wonder. Only one day into our escape and we were worn out. The moon that hovered overhead had hold of the water. We were on a boat smaller than a speck in the sky, small enough to be moved by its will. I'm sure the moon watched the whole thing happen, how we slept and how the knot became untied and how the boat drifted for the dark rim of shore.

CHAPTER SIXTEEN

Another Sideshow Attraction

I would like to blame the moon, but I can't. I would like to blame a mermaid for untying us, but I can't.

Wanda and I woke below a pier. The dory rubbed against one of the wooden support legs that walked through the water with the others like a centipede.

Wanda stirred, "What happened?"

"Oh no…" I sat up and the boat rocked. I moved around Wanda and I reached for the rope. It was loose as an empty fishing line. I let it go slack. "I must have tied a granny knot," I admitted. My back was killing me—Wanda's too by the look of her—sleeping on a wooden floor will do that to you.

"Brrr!" Wanda tugged her jacket on.

"I know. There must be a better way to hide from a tiger." I used an oar to push us out of the cold shadows. A fish might have liked lurking under here, but I steered for the gray daylight.

A float was parked beside the pier. It had a rusted, slanted, dilapidated look. It must have been treading water there for years.

Wanda reached out as we swung in and she took hold of a cleat and gagged. The float looked like the newspapered bottom of a seagull cage. Quick as she could, Wanda roped us to it then plunged her hands into the lake to wash them off.

I drawled like a millionaire, "For you my dear, nothing but the finest accommodations." As she stepped out of our yacht, I offered my hand to steady her. The setting we found ourselves in reminded me of the big painting we left at Geppetto's. I could picture that same peg-leg sailor sawing logs by the ramp Wanda scurried for. I followed the Beck patch as she shot up like a rocket.

Once we were topside, I recognized the boardwalk we were on: it was Pier 56. The penny arcades weren't open yet. The crowds from the night before left a trail of crushed cigarettes, paper cups, hotdog wrappers the seagulls cried over. The merry-go-round at the end of the dock was a dead flower. It would wheeze back to life again tonight. I leaned against the arcade wall to tug on the heel of my shoe. It felt like a periwinkle had crawled inside.

Ahead of me, Wanda made her way towards the only sign of life besides the scrabbling gulls: a two wheeled wooden cart where a man in an apron leaned. A couple coffee urns steamed. I agreed with her—a nice cup of hot coffee would do wonders—then I froze. I tried to yell her name. A big animal was reined to the front of the cart. A big striped animal! It took me another moment to process the picture. Sometimes that moment is all you have between life and death. Just ask any deer in the headlights...Funny how your existence can click on such a moment. Then the telegram arrived. It was just a zebra I was seeing. Or a horse painted to look like one. Another sideshow attraction in a town full of them.

CHAPTER SEVENTEEN

Breakfast

I took a step towards Wanda and the coffee just as something scurried out of the arcade wall in my direction. Instantly I was in fight-or-flight mode again. How much more of this could my poor mortal body withstand? This time it was a rat. Not the sort you would expect to see roaming a waterfront carnival, this was a white rat, the kind they sold in pet stores like Talking Pet.

It stopped in front of me and stared. It looked like somebody's lost animal. It wanted my attention but it didn't seem able speak. I thought all pets could talk? Still, it looked me in the eyes and made a motion of writing. This rat came to the right person—I always carry a pen and paper. It's part of my trade. You never know where or how inspiration will strike.

"You want to tell me something?" I asked.

It nodded urgently and held out its slender hands while I bent down with a pen and my pocket notebook, opened to a blank page. I held that so it could write. It did pretty well for a rat. We were near a sort of circus after all, I shouldn't be surprised. When it was done, I stood up and turned the page around so I could read the message:

Your life is in danger. Tiger!

I've never been a fan of rats. They're in all the walls of the ghetto where I live. But I felt sure this one was trying to help. I told it, "Thank you," and I looked behind me, back down the long pier towards the avenue and for the third time in a row, my heart stopped.

The tiger! It was only a couple hundred feet away, maybe closer, taking its own sweet time. Though its wide body ambled lazily, its shiny eyes stabbed me, seized me.

"Don!" Wanda revived me.

I trotted backwards, then turned and ran towards her. What was I going to do, throw myself over her in hope the tiger would be satisfied eating only me?

Wanda grabbed a paper bag from the seller and scampered for the merry-go-round. What was she going to do, scare the tiger away with calliope? I was afraid to look behind me—if I saw the tiger about to pounce, I would die on the spot.

The vendor of the wagon scrambled atop his cart as I ran past. I splashed across a wide puddle. If I couldn't help Wanda, what good was I? At any second I expected claws to knock me down but I kept running to where Wanda stood, her back to the pier railing, with nothing but deep water beyond. She grabbed my hand and pulled me close.

The tiger was distracted by the vending cart. Ignoring the screams of the man holding the tilted umbrella up there, it inhaled the air, as if drinking in the coffee vapor, looking hungry for something more. It seemed to contemplate hopping onto the rickety structure, eating that man and picking its teeth with the umbrella when it was done. Tail flicking contently. If it did, that would give us time to slip away, maybe back to our dory tied below. An awful thing to think, I agree, but we didn't get the chance to see it occur. With a shake of its head, the tiger returned its attention to us and as it slapped through the puddle I took a protective step in front of Wanda. I told her, "If it gets me, you'll have time to run."

The tiger stopped a leap away from us and grinned and said, "My two devoted companions." Its sharp mouth smiled. "Or should I say, breakfast."

Then I heard the paper bag crackle and Wanda yelled, "Look, tiger! Two fresh donuts!" She waved them over her head, the tiger crouched—it all happened so fast—and the tiger leaped as she threw them over the railing. A musty orange rush soared between me and Wanda. It was like a city taxi cab. It hit the water twenty feet away and made a huge splash below. I don't know if it got the donuts.

Probably.

They were gone. For a moment we could see the tiger sink. A brighter blur in the green water as it disappeared. Some bubbles and ripples creased the surface, then calm.

Wanda said, "Wow."

"It sunk like a stone."

Somewhere in the weeds of the lake bottom, a tiger had been anchored.

Wanda squeezed my hand. "You were pretty brave standing in front of me. You were like Hadrian Beck."

"I wasn't, *you* were! That was smart of you to buy those donuts. How did you know that would work?"

"You said they were his weakness."

I shook my head. Some weakness…We watched the water. I guessed we were free.

The zebra pulled the cart around quickly towards land, bells, and clop, clop, clop, fading away.

CHAPTER EIGHTEEN

Carol

We also returned to land. We were anxious to leave Northlake Way. You won't receive a postcard from us saying wish you were here.

Walking away from Pier 56 took us across the street into a parking lot filled with boats. It was like low tide for the fishing fleet. Some of them had been stuck in the air for years. Moss grew on them, sparrows made nests in the masts. We were only a current winding through, one that flowed quietly and fast to the back fence where we poured out a tear. We were done with the lake and the things of the sea. Just like Dale Muldoon's painting, we were ready to cling to the land.

I wanted to ask Wanda something but I was afraid it would sound crazy. Crazy as Patsy Cline. I asked her anyway, "Did you recognize the tiger's voice?" I was chilled just thinking about it. I looked at the ground.

Someone else used this same path we were on. The dirt and weeds were padded down. Whoever else it was also looked for shortcuts and liked to avoid the streets like us...a deer that would go to the lake to drink, or a ghost who dragged their feet at night.

I never recognized the speech of an animal before...

until that tiger.

"It was Herman Paxter," Wanda said. "What does it mean if that's true?"

I don't know but I liked her eyes under that fedora.

Dandelions flowered like traffic lights along the corridor. Wanda stopped and pointed at a nearby patch of them, to where a black rabbit was crying.

It rubbed its eyes and told us, "This happens to every friend I know." Another rabbit was lying beside it, dead by the looks of it. It *was* dead, on its side, staring marble eyes at the sky.

Wanda said, "What happened?"

"A tiger." The rabbit could have pressed a button that put us in deep freeze. The rabbit took a breath and went on, "It made a lot of noise. We knew it was coming, but we were busy talking to each other. It killed Carol for no reason, just swatted her as he went to the lake. He murdered her!"

"He was going to the lake?"

The rabbit moved its arms like a train. "Huffing and puffing."

"And you haven't seen him again?"

"Are you kidding me? If he returns I'll be the next to go! A rabbit's life isn't worth a cent."

A bird landed next to us. Another bit of research I've done for *Plot Command* left me with the knowledge of birds. I knew it was a junco. It asked us, "Hear about the tiger?"

We said yes together. Then it turned out the little

bird knew us. Maybe birds studied people the way birdwatchers studied them. "You're the people the tiger was hunting!"

Wanda admitted we were. Apparently we were the talk of the animal world.

The bird chirped, "Herman Paxter will send another one after you! He won't stop until he gets you!"

The rabbit told us, "You guys are worse off than me!" It turns out all the animals have been buzzing like telephone lines talking about us. The rabbit crossed its arms, "You're in big trouble!" and the bird agreed.

As if that meaning suddenly dawned on them, they sprinted and flew away from us. We must have become Bonnie and Clyde.

It was my idea to bury the rabbit's friend before we left. We couldn't leave it there. I don't know what animals do with their dead. I've seen crows keeping guard over one where it crashed. Elephants go to a jungle graveyard. Old pets crawl away. This one ended up in a shallow grave under blackberry thorns. Wanda placed some bluebells on top and a yellow flower I don't know the name for.

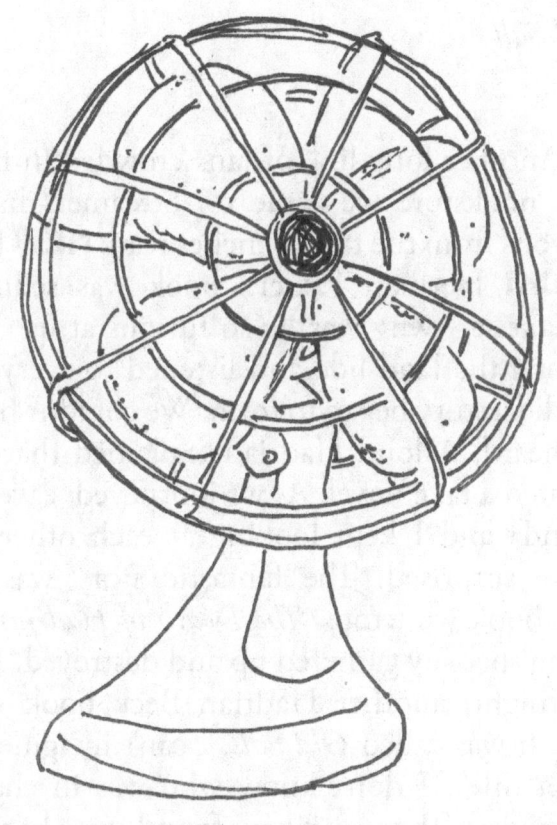

the talk of the animal world

CHAPTER NINETEEN

Old Salt

    Another long line of fans crowded in front of the first bookstore we came to. Streamers hanging like crayons from the tree branches read: **NEW HADRIAN BECK!** Herman Paxter's book was selling like an avalanche—why was he so furious at us? We walked among the landslide and listened to everyone and as we did a story began to form. We couldn't believe what he heard. A loud Hadrian explained that insurgents printed a fake novel. As we journeyed, eavesdropping, Wanda and I kept looking at each other more and more surprised. The fantastic story was filling in. The book we wrote, *The Death of Hadrian Beck*, was being speedily gathered up and destroyed. In its place, overnight, another Hadrian Beck book was rushed out. It was called *Old Salt*. I can't imagine using that for a title…I don't know who was in charge of the typewriter. They must have found some hack, someone who had no problem typing in the same old words.

    The sidewalk turned the corner and we followed. We were drifting across the radio dial, everyone had something to say. I was overjoyed to overhear a girl say she liked our Beck book, but when I tugged Wanda's green jacket so she could listen, the girl caught us staring and went silent. I looked away quickly—I didn't want to alarm her. The country was at war and you had to be careful what you said. We stopped by the curb in front of the store. Posters of the book's cover art filled the widow like church stain glass panels.

"It's Dale's painting!" we both gasped.

It was the same one we hung on the wall at Geppetto's yesterday! Now it had *Old Salt* scrimshawed across it.

"Come on, let's go inside," Wanda started for the door, proclaiming, "Excuse me, we're from the *Herald*," as we shoved against the line into the store. Everyone else channeled past a table stacked tall with *Old Salt* on their way to the register. We were all swept up in the excitement. I was watching someone who just bought a copy. She tucked it in her arms. There were more people like her too who stood off to the side and were already reading.

Wanda pointed, "Look!" Against the wall stood a listening booth—you could pay three dollars and hear three minutes worth of *Old Salt* read to you. "Do you have $3?"

I still had my wallet. I couldn't be sure if there was anything in it. I once had an inchworm ask me if it could rent room in there. By some miracle though, I had a five dollar bill. Nobody was using the booth so we went in and paid the meter. Wanda shut the door. The space was no bigger than a phone booth, made for one listener at a time, but we didn't mind being near.

I held the headphones between our ears and we heard a sandpapery voice announce, "*Old Salt*, a Hadrian Beck novel by Herman Paxter." The typewriter didn't waste any time telling the story, the action rolled right down the track. Hadrian Beck washes ashore in a lifeboat. He has no memory of how he arrived, only a burning thirst for revenge…When our three minutes ended it was clear Hadrian was back without any knowledge of the life he lived in the condemned book that we wrote. I set the headphones on the narrow shelf and opened the door for Wanda.

We stared at all those Hadrian Beck fans and Wanda said, "They're going to love it, aren't they?" But I wondered about that girl we overheard. How many were like her? It was hard to tell. They were the quiet ones. I said, "Let's get out of here."

We didn't get too far, only to the end of the block when Dale Muldoon appeared. He grinned and bellowed, "Did you see the book? Did you see my painting on the cover?"

I wanted to ask him why it was his painting when it was painted by a kid with only a mop to his name. But what was the point? We were all in the same boat. What I should have asked him—what I did ask Wanda once we were alone again, walking—was, "How did the tiger know where we would be? Who told it we would be across the street in a pizzeria?"

Wanda looked at me like I was crazy when I asked

her.

I said, "Okay then, but why is Muldoon's painting on the cover of Paxter's book? Isn't that a bit suspicious?"

She didn't think so. Dale was her friend, he had connections, and he was a well known artist. I felt bad about bringing it up. Where was that peddler with the flowers now?

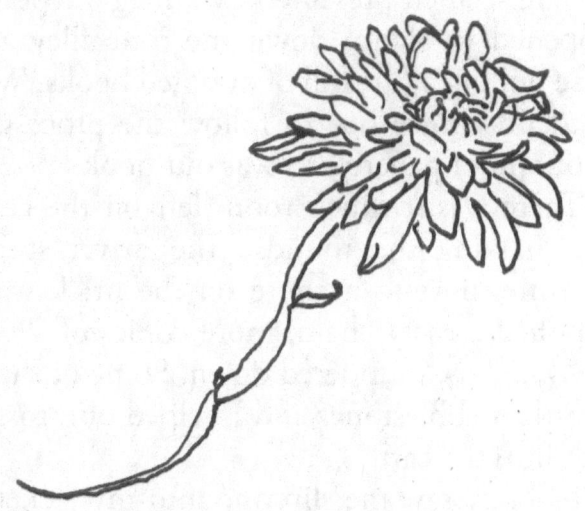

The same pandemonium greeted us at the bookstore on the next corner. I was still thinking about Dale Muldoon—maybe Wanda was right about his innocence—after all, he did help with our book. He was no different than us: he just wanted his work to be seen. He had a vision to share with the world…and there it was in every shop window—a million peg-leg sailors.

CHAPTER TWENTY

One of Many

As a writer, I had to admire the timing. Once again our fate seemed presented by a magic typewriter. We happened to glance down the next alley and saw a horse pulling a cart full of doomed books. Wanda and I had no choice but to follow the procession. That mountain of paperbacks was our book.

There wasn't much room left on the cart. It had been making the rounds. The driver stopped one last time, next to a chute on the brick wall. When he pulled a rusty chain, more copies of *The Death of Hadrian Beck* thundered down. Some of them spilled onto the cobblestones and I helped out, tossing them back into the cart.

Nobody saw me slip one into my jacket. A thief! No, I prefer to think I was saving one book at least for history. Someday someone would be glad I did. It felt like the funeral procession of an American hero, the steady clop of the hooves and the slow creaking wheels. Wanda and I plodded along with it. There was nothing to say.

The driver didn't have much to say either, not to us anyway. He and his horse though knew each other for so long they could carry on a conversation with just a few well polished words.

Usually by this time I'd be writing ideas for the next book. What was I supposed to do with my notebook now?

As the alley emptied out, our destination became clear. Wanda covered her mouth. Other wagons were arriving at the Cascade Bank parking lot with us. Books were dumped into a heap in the middle of the tar. Packs of Hadrians roamed in the crowd. I stopped and took Wanda's hand. I remembered those boys who caught us with the manuscript two days ago. I told Wanda I bet they would remember us—and it wouldn't be a family reunion.

We stayed where we were, at a safe distance across the street with a telephone pole next to us. If another tiger showed, we could climb the rungs.

A few yards from us, a crumpled old man was reading aloud from *Old Salt*. On another day he might be seen pacing the sidewalk with a sign telling everyone the sky is falling.

More people were filling the parking lot and sidewalk and cars were passing, slow as turtle taxis. With the fellow barking *Old Salt* in our ears and all the roar of commotion around us it was turning more and more into a circus. A banner was unrolled **BONFIRE TONIGHT!** and caused a shout of approval.

No, it wasn't a good idea for us to be seen here and I was reaching for Wanda to tell her that when a car shot across the lane, aimed for our corner. It knocked against a scrap merchant's wagon and I barely had time to pull Wanda back as it bucked over the curb and slammed into the telephone pole.

Behind the cracked windshield, holding onto the wheel, a tiger slumped. The cowboy hat it wore tipped over its eyes but I knew we were its target. The telephone wires shook and swung overhead, the car's cracked engine block steamed, the tiger leaned off the horn. It might have been struggling to get out—we didn't wait to find out.

"Here we go again!" I cried, "Run!"

I heard Wanda say, "I thought tigers were rare!"

As we bolted, we separated around a rug seller and met again like a river. "Why was it driving?" Wanda said.

I've noticed that before. Sometimes you see animals trying to do things that people do. Especially since they started talking and got closer to our ways. They didn't always succeed. Driving was something they failed at spectacularly. They kept trying though. That tiger with its cowboy hat was one of many. I don't think either one of us wished it harm—there was already one tiger at the bottom of the lake—we just wanted them to leave us alone. It would be nice to go home. We had to find new jobs too. Imagine walking into the office again as if nothing happened, and starting to work on a new book. Herman Paxter probably had the typewriter wired to explode if I tried.

Scaffolding ahead, we ran across the street. We

could have jumped onto the platform of a trolley if the ticket collector wasn't watching us. A Laundromat caught my eye. I thought about us hiding in there, under a basket full of warm sheets.

A car horn nipped the air.

The red American Driving School sedan pulled to the curb and the driver called out the open window, "You're running again!"

"We never stopped," said Wanda.

"Well hop in."

We did. We were happy to.

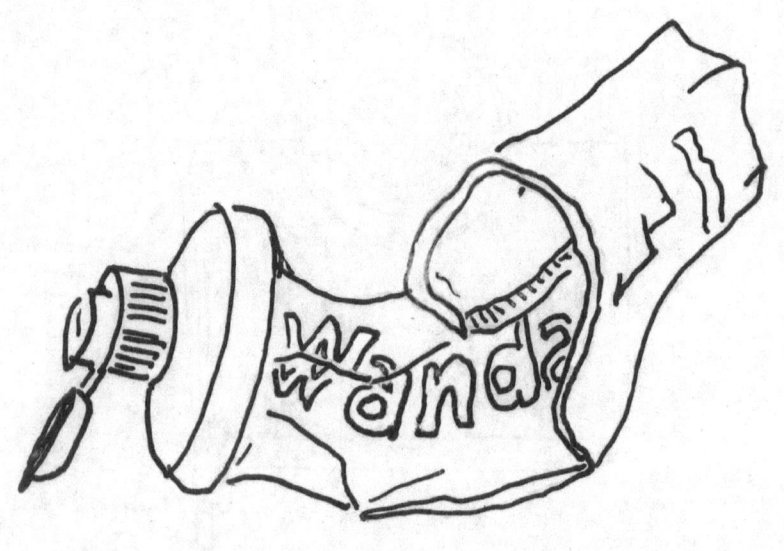

there's so little I know

CHAPTER TWENTY ONE

Escaping

"You remember Thelma?"

Of course we did, we were out of breath elated to see her again. She could have been the Lone Ranger.

While Thelma steered the car into the flow of traffic, I looked out the back window. It was okay. No tiger limping after us. Maybe the accident had knocked some sense into it. Maybe it left the crashed car and went for a stroll in the arboretum to reassess its life. On a sunny park bench it had an epiphany and thought, "What am I doing in a city? This isn't my dream." It tipped back its cowboy hat and decided it was time for those wide open plains where the deer and the antelope play.

Our speed picked up the further we got from tonight's witch burning. Thelma was improving.

"What are you escaping this time?" the instructor asked us, "Gangsters?"

"Worse," Wanda told him.

"Worse than gangsters?"

"Another tiger wants to kill us," she blurted. "We're running out of options too." Suddenly she was only a paintbrush away from shipwreck tears, drowning in the green sea of her army jacket and soggy brimmed fedora. I should have put my arm around her. We were close enough I could do that. But I didn't know what to do either. I only write books, there's so little I know about the real world.

The instructor leaned over the vinyl seat and confided, "A cousin of mine got chased by a tiger. It happens more often than you think. *Eyes on the road, Thelma!*" With a jerk, the car corrected itself and he continued solemnly, "He didn't stand a chance on his own…" He glanced at the road then back to us. "This is about your survival. There's only one way I know to get out of this kind of trouble."

"What? What is it?" Wanda asked desperately.

"We just want to go home," I added. That's right—I missed the slums of 32nd Street.

He told Thelma, "Turn at the next traffic light," then he shot me a look and said, "I'm afraid you've lost that chance." The car was slowing. Thelma was mumbling. He asked us seriously, "Are you really ready to disappear? Because that's what you'll have to do if you want to live."

CHAPTER TWENTY TWO

Midas Watts

Midas Watts was expecting us. No wonder. The American Driving School delivered us to an all-knowing mystic. My first thought was here's someone who will transmigrate our souls into another part of the world. I wasn't far off. He directed us to chairs by a curtained window. He kept out the sight of the tenements with thick red drapes the sunlight had to sift its way through. He smiled, "I've been watching you. I've been helping you as much as I could. It's good that you're here." His smile remained as he sat across from us. "We can't afford to lose any more tigers." No, no, of course not, we were all in agreement on that, but Midas Watts' suggestion was difficult to imagine. He told us about a place we could hide, a sort of Noah's ark as it turned out. Did we have a choice? Did Noah? Not if we wanted to survive. I didn't have any trouble agreeing with Wanda when she told Midas we were ready to go.

Perhaps it would be more thrilling to say we were guided to a door behind a tapestry, one that led to a subterranean tunnel where a carriage awaited in the alley, windows blacked out. But that isn't what happened. Midas Watts said, "Follow me please."

We weren't going into the seams of the city, Midas halted beside a ladder. Like a magic beanstalk, it stepped from this basement floor up into the ceiling. Midas pointed and smiled. I don't know if that smile ever left. It would probably stay down here glowing like a jack o' lantern.

And wasn't I brave as Hadrian Beck, offering to go first? If there was a tiger upstairs wearing a bib I would be first on the menu.

I don't remember the last time I climbed a ladder. This was a memorable one though, especially since it might be my last ladder. That would be a good Hadrian Beck title: *The Last Ladder*. My fingers itched to write that down.

Before I knew it I was emerging through the ceiling onto an office floor. I stepped off on the blue carpeting.

There wasn't much to the room. A round desk in the middle, with two chairs facing each other. A door set in one wall. "It's okay, Wanda!" I didn't need to shout—she was already standing behind me. "It's like our old office."

"After Mary Poppins paid a visit."

I laughed, picturing her hovering, umbrella in hand.

Wanda said, "There's our desk."

"Looks just like Midas told us. All we need to do is take a seat." We were here to audition for Midas or whoever was in charge and if we passed...well, we would see. A new life with Talking Pet was better than being killed off by a tiger. I moved towards the table. No typewriter, no paper, it would be an adjustment. I sat and stared at Wanda across from me. Before either of us could speak, the lights began to dim.

The show at the wax museum on Pier 56 begins the same way—I half expected The Beatles to materialize along the wall. As we seemed to seep into underwater darkness, above us two halos of pale blue light descended, slowly, settling one above Wanda and one above me.

I watched the halo hover in the air just inches over Wanda's head. I couldn't move though, I couldn't speak. I wasn't afraid of the warm glow but I wondered about the strange technology. Why had I never heard of this invention before? Maybe it had nothing to do with machinery. It was a ghostly thing.

Wanda's eyes closed sleepily. I felt mine shutting too. We were so tired…Our running was over…I felt good. Another world was waiting.

WHIPPET - Male, unneutered. 1 - 3 yrs. Found 54th & Keystone Pl. N on 3/4/91. Call

what we used to be

CHAPTER TWENTY THREE

Safeway

What do I see? A girl's face got close to mine as a pinwheel. She asked me something, she's waiting to hear my answer. Those shiny eyes of hers are waiting. I had to do something…then I remembered what Midas Watts told us. The world would seem strange at first. We had to whole heartedly become whatever others wanted of us. What we used to be will have vanished without a trace. Now we were working for Talking Pet.

I had to say something so I blurted cartoonishly, "Hiya, kiddo."

She was delighted. "You can talk!"

"Of course I can. Anything special you want to talk about?"

"Bugs."

"Bugs! Insects? Let's see…Well, I had a heck of a time with ants in my doghouse last spring."

She shrieked with laughter. I never saw anything like it. We could be a star act on The Sylvan Moore Show.

She hugged me. "Safeway, you're funny!"

"What? *Safeway?*"

"That's your name, remember? I got you from that

apple box outside Safeway. I took you home and Dad said we could get you to talk if we went to Talking Pet and it worked!"

Safeway...I was named for a grocery store chain. Fortunately I didn't remember that cruel beginning of mine. Everything from this point was brand new.

Inez had a nice room. I could tell she was well cared for, she had every comfort she needed and artwork on the walls, and all her favorite things told a story about her. I could tell she liked dogs. She had pictures of dogs, toys of them, dog books on the shelf, and a plush dog toy I wouldn't mind chewing on.

She took me for a walk and that was the best feeling. The world was almost overwhelming. I must have lost that feeling a long time ago when I was Don Wilson, office worker. Someone in the park was sitting on a bench, reading from a book while his dog stood next to him, talking. I watched the dog hop onto the bench and look over the man's shoulder. I suppose it's only a matter of time before Talking Pet dogs are reading too. We went past the baseball field, outside the fence in the grass. Being a dog, everything smelled unbelievable, so alive and great. I was excited to be here and the strangest memory arrived like one of those city buses I'd love to chase. I told her, "I used to play a little baseball when I was a boy." I was a catcher.

"What?"

I shouldn't have said that. Pets can't let on you're

really a person suspended in limbo at Talking Pet. Pet owners aren't supposed to know. I was quick to cover it up. I found a baseball by the track and I growled and peeled off the shell with my teeth. She tried to take it from me and I ran out of her reach. I heard the clink of a ball being hit. I let her get close to me then I jumped away again.

I had no problem keeping up with an eight year old. I guess that's because I was about the same age in dog years. We ran in circles, we got into mischief, we got hungry, we had tantrums and we grew exhausted until we finally needed a nap. Last thing I saw was Inez's mother closing the door as quietly as possible. From the look on her face, you would have thought we were escaped convicts who fell asleep in a barn.

CHAPTER TWENTY FOUR

Gorilla Experience

Next I knew I was waking up in that bare office again. Wanda was awake again too. She rubbed her eyes and yawned. I remembered part of my dream, chasing a cat up a tree. The rest of it was fading away.

"I must have been sleeping," Wanda said.

The lights were on again and the halos or whatever they were had gone.

She asked, "Did you dream you were an animal?"

"I think so."

She told me about flying around inside a cage, talking away like a radio and I told her I remembered talking too. She laughed when I told her I was a dog.

We both got quiet though when we saw Midas Watts rise from the floor like a smiling genie. He greeted us and he congratulated us, "You did very well."

Neither one of us was quick to acknowledge his compliment. What had we done—behaved in a dream world?

He told us, "Talking Pet approves your employment."

That's right, that wasn't a dream world. We had been talking pets somewhere in this real world.

Midas Watts was offering us new lives as animals. We passed the test. It didn't seem that difficult. In fact, I already had a little experience. One time I borrowed a friend's gorilla costume. It was all folded up neatly in a suitcase—a black fur body with separate hands, feet and a head. Nobody paid any attention to me as I walked to the library like that and checked out *Imminent Contagion* then walked home again. Although I was surprised at the time that I could slip so unnoticed among all those people, now I saw it as my natural ability to play the part to perfection.

So with nowhere else to go, Wanda and I agreed to his terms and Midas Watts gave us contracts to sign. I never saw one like it before. The paper was divided into four squares with a line drawing of an animal in each section. All we had to do was mark 1-4 in order of preference. I chose (1) OWL (2) SEAL (3) COW (4) SEAGULL.

Midas took our contracts and asked us to walk with him. I wondered what animals Wanda wrote down, but I didn't get a chance to ask.

Midas stopped by the door I noticed before. "This way to your new life..." He turned the handle and pulled the door open.

CHAPTER TWENTY FIVE

Talking Pet

Talking Pet filled the gloom of a room big as a garage for the Hindenburg. Hundreds of people sat in long rows of tables, a nimbus of light over each sleeping person. We could tell where our stations were. Out of all those blue halos, two were blinking red. The floated a little higher than the others. At least we wouldn't be far from each other when we sat down. It was spooky being the only ones with awareness. Like walking through a cemetery, we didn't want to wake anyone.

Wanda took her seat. The halo above her turned blue and began to fall.

"Oh—" I said, remembering what I wanted to ask her, "What animal did you pick?" I had to take a step back from the glowing hoop before it struck me. I quickly added, "Maybe I can find you in my dream. I'll look for you."

She never got the chance to answer. Her eyes were closed. Those halos really knocked you out fast.

Mine was waiting a couple chairs away from her. I stayed near Wanda. I wasn't ready to leave her. I didn't want to be in some other world happening without her. I promised I would do my best to find her. Once

I was an owl, I could call her name deep into the night and fly past every window in town, looking. Don't worry.

Everyone, every dim shadow in this room was a talking animal, breathing in a different somewhere. Two chairs away from Wanda, I sat and waited for that blue crown to come down.

Suddenly there was no ground under my feet. I was lying on the wind, spinning slow in a smooth porcelain cup. My arms were wings. They carried me free of the clouds and I recognized our town spread below. Sparks of sunlight on the water, boats, little cars crossing the bridge to land. State Street ran along the shore. I turned my head, buffeted, and I could see where the slums were thrown on 32nd. I don't know how to describe this flying feeling. You might remember the elation as a kid, sometimes on a swing, or a Ferris wheel ride, but there's no way a person can be a bird except in a dream.

Before something could happen—I knew it would, something always did—I called out, "Waa—aa—aanda! Raa-aa—aamone!" Right away that sound told me I was no owl.

Of course the white shape of my sharp wings was all wrong and my voice was a shriek. Wasn't seagull my last choice on the contract? Where was the justice in that?

Oh, I guess it makes sense. Part of me has always been tied to them. I never strayed far from where

a haunted kite

seagulls are. They wander in the gray air above me or watch from building tops, parking lots. They're more dream than me and when you see one up close: a ghost, a haunted kite, someone's stoppered drop of soul the water stole away. I was meant to be this bird.

What are we always looking for? I couldn't say for the rest of the seagulls chasing fishing boats or screaming on rocks. I let the airstream carry me towards the earth.

I remembered Wanda Ramone.

It was funny that I would start this new life remembering so much about my last—there was Boulevard Park, the factory, the streets I used to walk, the bench where Wanda read our book, the café I went to with her. There was a lot to miss and this new life was just beginning. I went lower and I could read words on billboards and buildings. Nothing had changed, only me.

I circled the nine-story Leopold apartments, saw myself in the windows, and I was joined by another seagull loitering in the air nearby. It came closer and screeched, "Where the food at?" It came back around again and I had to swerve. "Food?" it yelped.

I flew away from it. I didn't want to talk again. It was hard to get used to that sound—my voice felt raw as an old tin can. Even flying round the city was getting routine, like holding on to a subway strap.

Another gull spotted me and veered away from the railroad tracks. I quickly twisted and found a new direction. I wasn't interested in answering their questions. I had other things on my mind. Really only one…There was only one Wanda Ramone. It's a town full of animals, some tame, some wild, and everyone is looking for something. Even if Wanda Ramone was only a ladybug on a dandelion leaf, we would find each other. I promised.

As I followed Donovan Ave inland I realized it was the way I used to go when I wanted to go home, only now I was looking at it like a map from the sky. I was pretty good at flying by now. I could have been a natural. If only I still had my notebook and pen, I could tell the world what it was like to be an extraordinary seagull. It was too bad I couldn't write. In this life I have a different purpose.

CHAPTER TWENTY SIX

The Life of a Hungry Ghost

I was much lower, not much higher than the treetops and the telephone wires, as I banked sharply to the left. 32nd Street unrolled, unfolding past houses and gardens towards the slums at the end. A strange destination for me as a seagull—was I going to let myself into my apartment? What would a bird need from there that nature didn't already provide? It could be that Wanda had the same plan, that we both head back home like salmon. I just hope she isn't a goldfish or a rabbit locked in a hutch. How on earth was I going to find her if she was someone's trapped pet? At least I seemed to be free to look for her.

I hit a rough patch in the air, like a whorl in a board of pine. I flapped but there was no escaping gravity, I was going down. Narrowly avoiding the electric lines above the sidewalk, I landed on the roof of a small blue house.

My big yellow feet planted like rubber boots on the pitch and walked me a few steps while I tucked my wings away and stopped not far from the chimney. It was a new life for me here but it also felt familiar. Before Don Wilson took over its controls, this was that seagull's home sweet home. I sat on the peak and sighed. Apparently this was where I belonged.

I blinked and watched down the steep shingles as a bicycle passed. What if I blinked again and all those memories of my other life suddenly washed away? Somehow I had to remember that the real me was asleep, Wanda Ramone was only two chairs to my left, and we were just working for Talking Pet. That's right, and we could pass the word along to all the ferocious animals and ask to be left alone. If we could do that, we could be ourselves again. That must be why smiling Midas Watts sent me here. I had to tie up some loose ends for the next life awaiting me.

Thinking that made me feel better. Birds were chatting in the yard. I heard what they're saying, plain as day. That would be another interesting thing for my notebook.

A screen door hidden from my view opened and all of a sudden I was hungry. This bird body had a life before me, it knew where it was meant to be, and it led me automatically. I stood and greeted the old man who tottered onto the grass below.

He looked up at me and waved. He was holding a fish by the tail. "You ready for your supper?"

I was. I held out my wings for balance as the fish flipped towards me and slapped on the roof. I acted quickly. The roof was a frozen wave and I slanted across it and swallowed the fish whole. That's how we do things—seagulls aren't known for their etiquette—forget about manners. I already heard the noxious cry of another of my kind wailing in the sky. Its shriek was joined by another. Amazing how fast the word gets around when there's food to be had. That's the life of a hungry ghost. Three seagulls wheeled over me and rained abuse. One even landed on the chimney and glared.

"Thank you!" I called out to the old man. I supposed I must be his pet. It's true, that's what I was. I could tell when he gave a laugh and replied, shading his eyes, "You can talk now! It worked!"

I saluted with my wing and bowed, "Say, I'm curious. How much does one spend to get an animal talking?" To my horror, I sounded like Cary Grant. Something seemed to be wrong with my transformation. Was there a voice button someone pressed by accident?

He told me hesitantly, "200 clams."

CHAPTER TWENTY SEVEN

Cary Grant

I repeated the amount, "Two hundred clams?" The way I spoke, you would have thought I just stepped off a yacht in Harvard Square, "Well, I must say I'm most appreciative. I genuinely am." I grinned, or tried to. It wasn't easy with a beak.

The old man stared at me a long moment before saying, "Is that really how you talk?"

I chuckled, "Oh, that's rich, you slay me, you really do."

"Phewww…" the old man shook his head ruefully. "Worst mistake of my life getting you to talk," and he returned to his house, disappearing beneath the eaves before I could reply.

The door slammed.

That echo took a while to fill with birds, whispering at first then gossiping louder. Cars rushed on the distant interstate. What's wrong with sounding like Cary Grant?

I wasn't doing it on purpose either. I'm not one of those impressionist acts you see at The Show Off. I could be though. If I showed up at the café and delivered my lines, I would be a hit sensation. Next stop Broadway.

The telephone line shook and I imagined that

was the message leaving the old man's house, racing down the street towards Talking Pet headquarters, demanding his 200 clams back.

A squirrel jumped off the swinging wire into the nearby birch tree. That's why the line had been given life. Hadrian Beck idea: instead of telephone technology, people tie notes to squirrels. They run above the city from pole to pole on a network of connected wires. An ingenious plot evolves to turn them into terrorists.

The hungry seagull on the chimney cursed and took off.

"I feel like a pariah," I muttered aloud.

The leaves of the alder tree close to the house shook. Something moved through them. It was getting close and then that approaching squirrel leaped onto the roof. I heard it gasp when it landed. I wasn't sure if seagulls were supposed to be scared of squirrels.

She said, "I'm trying to find someone."

I searched my memory for that voice as Cary Grant answered for me, "Of course you are! Aren't we all?"

She gave me a look that I knew by heart.

We said each other's names in a collision.

"Isn't this remarkable!" I held my wings out for a hug and Wanda got lost in my feathers. I have to admit, she turned out to be someone to have an adventure with.

She asked, "What happened to your voice?"

"What can I say, my dear. I'm charming now."

learning to live with it

CHAPTER TWENTY EIGHT

A Brooklyn Tiger

Here I was walking along another roof, blocks from where we started, and looking at my flapping, bright yellow feet. I asked Wanda, "Did I tell you about my grandfather's big toe?"

She answered slowly, "Ummm, no…" her voice beaming from a gray squirrel.

I tried my best to control Cary Grant, but I'm afraid I was learning to live with it. "When I was, ohhh…let's say eleven or so, my grandfather had a very keen notion to let his toenail grow. So over the course of my summer holiday we would check on the old man's progress every week." Wanda made a face, but I continued, nonplussed, "You see, he saw a photograph of a swami in India that sparked his imagination. My grandfather was certain he could do the same thing."

Wanda hopped off the gutter. She caught a branch and scurried through the spring leaves. I flew to the next rooftop and waited for her. If only I could get us a car, I bet I could still drive, and we'd get there in no time at all.

I was excited to tell her what happened next in my story. Once he got going, Cary Grant got the better of me. I paced along the tar paper impatiently. Too bad Wanda wasn't a flying squirrel.

Then a voice interrupted that thought, "Well, well, well…what do we have here?"

Sidling up behind me came a striped orange cat and for a second I was terrified, thinking it was a tiger. The housecat saw the fear in my eyes and loved it. "What's the matter, dodo?"

Whoever was asleep back at Talking Pet was auditioning for a 1940s Hollywood movie, set on the docks of Brooklyn. All this cat needed was a cigarette and a slouch hat. "Seems to me you don't got no pass, do you?"

"A pass? Do I require a pass to walk across this lackluster roof?"

"Yeah," he bristled. "Yeah, maybe this roof ain't got no luster…" the cat stepped closer, "But it's *my* roof, see?" He tapped his chest with a paw. "And I choose who comes and goes."

"Oh, brother, if you don't take the cake and eat it too."

"Yeah?" he sneered at me.

"Yeah!" I mocked him back. Believe me, this wasn't me talking. I don't even think it was Cary Grant talking—it sounded like him though.

"Listen, flapper," the orange cat seethed, "I don't like you."

"Well the feeling is mutual." It looked like I was about to sink to his violent level when Wanda pounced on the roof.

"Now, now," she said, "No fighting. I'm sure you don't want me to overrun your roof with squirrels. There's hundreds of us out there and only one of you."

The cat cringed. Wanda put the scare in him. Still eyeing the tree suspiciously, he backed off from us. I wondered who this cat really was—he could be the guy sitting right next to me back in the factory. Then again, who was I to judge? A seagull from Bristol…

Wanda scampered along the ledge. Another tree held out branches to climb on. But as I was about to raise my wings, a thought occurred. I didn't have to leave things this way. I looked at the Brooklyn cat again. He was brooding by a big can of roofing tar. I said, "Sorry about insulting your roof, old man. I got hot under the collar. That was just careless talk. It's a fine roof. You deserve to be proud of it."

That took him by surprise. I don't think anyone ever complimented him. It wasn't in the script. Anyway, I didn't stick around for his next line. I was back in the sky.

CHAPTER TWENTY NINE

John Wayne

I had to duck a bee. The air is not just an empty space; it's filled with all manner of other flyers. It's a miracle we aren't bumping into each other all the time. Imagine being an air traffic controller for the sidewalk paths and streets, trying to direct all the butterflies, songbirds and falling leaves. Some unseen radar must be protecting us.

Wanda and I weren't just jumping from roof to roof at random, we did have a destination in mind and fortunately we weren't far. A seagull is faster than a squirrel to get there though. I would have to wait for her. I landed atop a glowing red and yellow neon sign and Cary Grant greeted it, "Geppetto's Pizzeria, we meet again."

This was Wanda's idea and her absence gave me time to think about it. I hoped it would work. Honestly, we weren't meant to be talking pets and if her plan worked we wouldn't need to be. And what if we did leave this dream? You should leave something good behind, break the mold, make a change like I did with that orange cat who was used to putting up a fight and lived to draw others into its web, and probably never heard a kind word. Maybe that spell had been broken. Maybe that rooftop cat had been transformed like Hadrian Beck.

From that signpost height, I could imagine something better. When I returned to life as Don Wilson I would remember. The world is real. We are the ones in a dream.

I let myself glide across the parking lot and landed on a phone booth. A thick wire ran from it to the nearest telephone pole. This was Step 1 of Wanda's plan. The phone booth was easy for her to find, just follow the lines leading to it. The glass booths popped up like flowers on the vine. Look for the one that smelled like pizza.

Another seagull loitered on the hood of a van, keeping an eye on me in case a fish was thrown at me. That was my reputation apparently. He was scowling. Did you know animals have a common language? One understood the whole world over like the sound of wind or rain. What he muttered wasn't poetry.

I watched a horse pulling a loaded cart. I thought they had a radio going. Then I realized it was the horse carrying on about the day's horse track results. Another wagon passed it, pulled by a goat. I had lots of time to reflect on the scene, the whirling goings on of all the creatures around me, stuck in it as if painted on.

When Wanda finally showed, sliding down the wire with the ease of rainwater, I was so pleased I tried to applaud. Wings aren't the same as hands though.

They flapped for her. That was a long journey here for a squirrel. Her heart ticked like a windup toy I could feel through my feathers when we hugged.

"Step 2," Wanda panted.

This would start to get difficult. We had to gain entrance to Geppetto's Pizzeria. I've worked in restaurants before. I know for a fact they don't take kindly to seagulls or rodents on the premises. Wanda had it figured out. She had been busy in her squirrel incarnation. She met a blue jay who knew Herman Paxter's pet bulldog. Cannon, the same dog we saw in the photograph every day at the office, was devoted to this restaurant. All we had to do was talk to him.

Luckily, nobody paid attention to a squirrel and a seagull crossing the parking lot, going around the back of the building.

Before we got there, Wanda stopped me with a paw. "Can you do any other voices?" she asked me. "Can you imitate John Wayne? Your Cary Grant is great, I like it, but we need a different voice for this place."

I shut my eyes. John Wayne…I had seen his movies of course. He had a parched drawl that looped in the air like a lasso. Believe it or not, when I was a kid, ten or so, I saw his yacht moored offshore. I can remember that postcard image. I looked for him on the deck, but the ship was no bigger than a toy.

I cleared my throat. With my eyes still closed, I imagined John Wayne on a black and white stagecoach.

Then I saw him in Technicolor. He always had a gun. "Perhaps if I had a cowboy hat…" Cary Grant was fading away.

I must have been hypnotizing myself. When I felt a Western brim fit my head, I didn't know it was a wilted leaf of lettuce Wanda found by the kitchen door. My eyes opened and I was ready to go. "What are we waiting for, Wanda?" With my wings, I hoisted my invisible gun belt. "Where's this bulldog I heard so much talk about?"

Wanda scratched on the door while I stood guard, keeping lookout from a garbage can lid in the alley.

A teenager wearing a red apron opened the door. He held a big cooking pan half full of soapy water. He looked down at the squirrel outside, paused as if he was considering throwing it on her. For his sake, I hoped he wouldn't try. John Wayne as a seagull is still John Wayne.

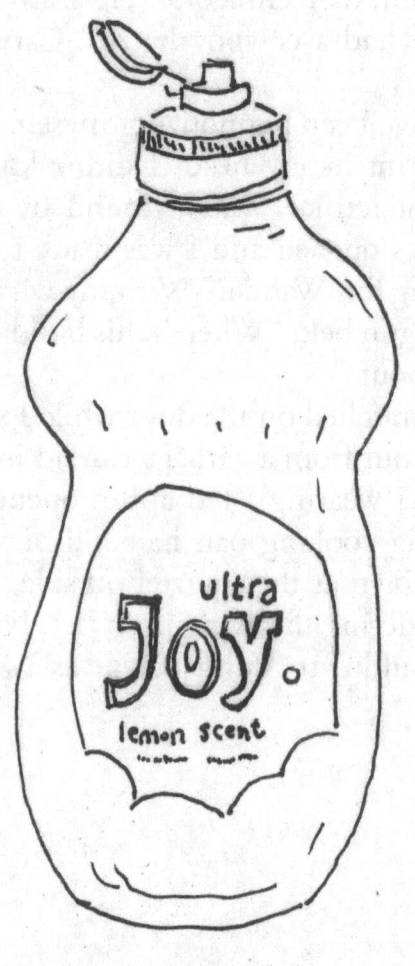

an important message

CHAPTER THIRTY

Prayer

Wanda rubbed her paws together like an urgent prayer, "We have an important message for one of your guests."

A fat soapy drop slopped and spotted the doorway. Go ahead, I tensed, just try and throw the rest of it...

Wanda begged, "Can we please speak with Cannon if he's here. It's urgent."

"I'll check." The pot of water withdrew. Along with it went the Dalton Gang and Jesse James. A tumbleweed breeze combed the alley.

"You reckon he's here?"

"That's what the blue jay told me," Wanda said. "Cannon eats here every day. He likes the calzone."

Stuck to our old office wall, the photo of Paxter and his bulldog floated in my memory. They looked like father and son.

With a worried squeak, Wanda told me, "Here comes Step 3."

I could hear Cannon's meaty feet slap the kitchen floor and then he showed his face behind the screen door. He wheezed, "I'm not signing autographs today."

"No, no it's not that, sir. We have a message for Mr. Paxter." Wanda twitched and pivoted towards me.

"I know you and Mr. Paxter are fans of John Wayne and this bird here—well, this seagull is John Wayne's reincarnation."

"That's right," I said, "pleasure to meet you, friend."

"Oh…" Cannon's jaw dropped. His knees wobbled, "I—my boss should be here! Can I run go call him?"

I held out a wing. "Steady, amigo. I don't have much time. I got a headwind out of town to catch. I just had to stop by to deliver a message before I leave."

"Of course, Mr. Wayne."

"Easy," I told him. "You can call me John."

"Yes, I will."

"Okay then. Here it is—there's a couple of real nice people your boss got it in for. I want Paxter to lay off. I want him to call off his posse. No more tigers. Alright?"

The bulldog sputtered, "I'll tell him, I'll call him right now, I'll let him know as soon as I can!"

I saluted with my wing as Cannon slammed the screen door in his hurry. Those feet of his sounded like a tractor with a flat tire.

Wanda ran her paw across her cheek. "Well, that's it! Step 3 is complete. I sure hope that worked!"

"Don't worry, ma'am. We did all we can." I flapped down from the garbage can lid and joined her.

"Oh, Don. Get that lettuce off your head."

It wasn't a Stetson anymore. What she swiped off of me crumpled on the cement like a tragic telegram. And with it went John Wayne.

She looked at me and smiled. "Let's find somewhere to fall asleep."

CHAPTER THIRTY ONE

Every Bee

What a strange thing, to wake up from feathers into skin. You could almost say I migrated back to myself. I looked to my left and saw Wanda stirring in the blue glow. Some people live the whole rest of their life as the animal they have become. They forget they are a person in a dream. But while everyone else slept, we willed ourselves awake.

It wasn't easy...Standing up felt like fighting the tide. I plodded over to Wanda and caught her as she stumbled from her chair.

"You're a person again," she whispered.

"So are you." I was glad for my arms, not wings, relieved to see that green Beck jacket she wore, happy to be with her most of all.

"Will we stay ourselves?"

I rubbed my neck. I wasn't sure. "Maybe we go back to animals when we fall asleep. I hope not. I know I'll feel better as soon as we get away from here though."

"Me too."

Nobody tried to stop us. I don't think anyone knew we were awake. The entire room was filled with dreams and we left the way we came in.

No sign of Midas Watts either. Nothing stood in front of the door. Outside in the air, Talking Pet became a blank brick wall.

It was morning in the alley where American Driving School dropped us off. The sky was a smooth blue gray light.

Right away I noticed Wanda had a halo. She pointed at me and said, "You do too!" True, we both had them. They hadn't gone away when we left our jobs at Talking Pet. I was ready to throw mine back at the bricks like a Frisbee, but when I reached up, my hand went through it.

Wanda laughed. She couldn't catch hers either.

So much for trying to sell them at a pawnshop! That might have bought us some breakfast. I was trying to be practical, the realistic one. I don't know how we're supposed to make a living out here looking this way. All Wanda needed was a harp and a pair of wings.

She said, "This is going to be interesting to try and explain."

"Well, I hope you're ready to try," I said. "Look…"

A deer was slowly approaching. Its long legs barely seemed to move as it neared, like a doe mounted on a sled pulled over snow.

"Hi," Wanda greeted it, "It sure is a nice morning."

The glassy eyes stared through us. We weren't invisible. I knew the deer could see us and its ears were cupped to catch our breath, but it didn't answer or betray any recognizable emotion. A deer on a hunting lodge wall could have been its regular day job.

Wanda's voice was still pleasant, "Are you going to Talking Pet? We just came from there."

All the deer needed was a peg-leg and it could have been a Dale Muldoon painting.

There wasn't anything unusual about a deer prowling the early morning streets. That's what they do. I've seen a lot in this town, here and there. Usually though, they have something to say. They bring news from wherever the trees remained: under bridges, underpasses, overgrown hollows or vacant lots. I like listening to them.

But sometimes you met an animal that couldn't talk. Talking Pet hadn't got to them yet. They were still natural and free. We realized this deer was one of them and Wanda gave our regards as we slipped by. Silently, we understood. We didn't need a reply. You couldn't hear little words from every passing bee.

OLD SALT
Written & Illustrated by Allen Frost
January-May 2020

about the author:

Allen Frost lives on 32nd Street near Bellingham Bay. He has written collections of poetry, essays, short stories, novels and is editor of Good Deed Rain books.

about the cover artist:

Leon Dusso (1918-1991) born in Los Angeles, began his artistic training with his father, who was an art director for Paramount Pictures. His oil paintings appeared in films, the *Perry Mason* TV series, as well as novels. This cover painting is currently for sale at Penny Lane antiques for $950.

Illustration from *Home Recordings* (2009)

Books by Good Deed Rain

Saint Lemonade, Allen Frost, 2014. Two novels illustrated by the author in the manner of the old Big Little Books.

Playground, Allen Frost, 2014. Poems collected from seven years of chapbooks.

Roosevelt, Allen Frost, 2015. A Pacific Northwest novel set in July, 1942, when a boy and a girl search for a missing elephant. Illustrated throughout by Fred Sodt.

5 Novels, Allen Frost, 2015. Novels written over five years, featuring circus giants, clockwork animals, detectives and time travelers.

The Sylvan Moore Show, Allen Frost, 2015. A short story omnibus of 193 stories written over 30 years.

Town in a Cloud, Allen Frost, 2015. A three part book of poetry, written during the Bellingham rainy seasons of fall, winter, and spring.

A Flutter of Birds Passing Through Heaven: A Tribute to Robert Sund, 2016. Edited by Allen Frost and Paul Piper. The story of a legendary Ish River poet & artist.

At the Edge of America, Allen Frost, 2016. Two novels in one book blend time travel in a mythical poetic America.

Lake Erie Submarine, Allen Frost, 2016. A two week vacation in Ohio inspired these poems, illustrated by the author.

and Light, Paul Piper, 2016. Poetry written over three years. Illustrated with watercolors by Penny Piper.

The Book of Ticks, Allen Frost, 2017. A giant collection of 8 mysterious adventures featuring Phil Ticks. Illustrated throughout by Aaron Gunderson.

I Can Only Imagine, Allen Frost, 2017. Five adventures of love and heartbreak dreamed in an imaginary world. Cover & color illustrations by Annabelle Barrett.

The Orphanage of Abandoned Teenagers, Allen Frost, 2017. A fictional guide for teens and their parents. Illustrated by the author.

In the Valley of Mystic Light: An Oral History of the Skagit Valley Arts Scene, 2017. Edited by Claire Swedberg & Rita Hupy.

Different Planet, Allen Frost, 2017. Four science fiction adventures: reincarnation, robots, talking animals, outer space and clones. Cover & illustrations by Laura Vasyutynska.

Go with the Flow: A Tribute to Clyde Sanborn, 2018. Edited by Allen Frost. The life and art of a timeless river poet. In beautiful living color!

Homeless Sutra, Allen Frost, 2018. Four stories: Sylvan Moore, a flying monk, a water salesman, and a guardian rabbit.

The Lake Walker, Allen Frost 2018. A little novel set in black and white like one of those old European movies about death and life.

A Hundred Dreams Ago, Allen Frost, 2018. A winter book of poetry and prose. Illustrated by Aaron Gunderson.

Almost Animals, Allen Frost, 2018. A collection of linked stories, thinking about what makes us animals.

The Robotic Age, Allen Frost, 2018. A vaudeville magician and his faithful robot track down ghosts. Illustrated throughout by Aaron Gunderson.

Kennedy, Allen Frost, 2018. This sequel to Roosevelt is a coming-of-age fable set during two weeks in 1962 in a mythical Kennedyland. Illustrated throughout by Fred Sodt.

Fable, Allen Frost, 2018. There's something going on in this country and I can best relate it in fable: the parable of the rabbits, a bedtime story, and the diary of our trip to Ohio.

Elbows & Knees: Essays & Plays, Allen Frost, 2018. A thrilling collection of writing about some of my favorite subjects, from B-movies to Brautigan.

The Last Paper Stars, Allen Frost 2019. A trip back in time to the 20 year old mind of Frankenstein, and two other worlds of the future.

Walt Amherst is Awake, Allen Frost, 2019. The dreamlife of an office worker. Illustrated throughout by Aaron Gunderson.

When You Smile You Let in Light, Allen Frost, 2019. An atomic love story written by a 23 year old.

Pinocchio in America, Allen Frost, 2019. After 82 years buried underground, Pinocchio returns to life behind a car repair shop in America.

Taking Her Sides on Immortality, Robert Huff, 2019. The long awaited poetry collection from a local, nationally renowned master of words.

Florida, Allen Frost, 2019. Three days in Florida turned into a book of sunshine inspired stories.

Blue Anthem Wailing, Allen Frost, 2019. My first novel written in college is an apocalyptic, Old Testament race through American shadows while Amelia Earhart flies overhead.

The Welfare Office, Allen Frost, 2019. The animals go in and out of the office, leaving these stories as footprints.

Island Air, Allen Frost, 2019. A detective novel featuring haiku, a lost library book and streetsongs.

Imaginary Someone, Allen Frost, 2020. A fictional memoir featuring 45 years of inspirations and obstacles in the life of a writer.

Violet of the Silent Movies, Allen Frost, 2020. A collection of starry-eyed short story poems, illustrated by the author.

The Tin Can Telephone, Allen Frost, 2020. A childhood memory novel set in 1975 Seattle, illustrated by author like a coloring book.

Heaven Crayon, Allen Frost, 2020. How *Ohio Trio* would look if printed as a Big Little Book. Illustrated by author.

Old Salt, Allen Frost, 2020. Authors of a fake novel get chased by tigers. Illustrations by author.

www.ingramcontent.com/pod-product-compliance
Lightning Source LLC
LaVergne TN
LVHW031540060526
838200LV00056B/4590